THE CASE OF THE

DAPPER DANDIE DINMONT

A Thousand Islands Doggy Inn Mystery

B.R. SNOW

Copyright © 2017 B.R. Snow
ISBN: 978-1-942691-10-5

Website: www.brsnow.net/
Twitter: @BernSnow
Facebook: facebook.com/bernsnow

Cover Design: Reggie Cullen
Cover Photo: James R. Miller

Other Books by B.R. Snow

The Thousand Islands Doggy Inn Mysteries

- The Case of the Abandoned Aussie
- The Case of the Brokenhearted Bulldog
- The Case of the Caged Cockers

The Damaged Po$$e Series

- American Midnight
- Larrikin Gene
- Sneaker World
- Summerman
- The Duplicates

Other books

- Divorce Hotel
- Either Ore

To JR and Kathy

Chapter 1

When it comes to winter in the Thousand Islands, I do my utmost best to remain philosophical. Especially by the time February rolls around. Over the years, winter has come to symbolize rebirth as Mother Nature performs her own often brutal version of hibernation bringing cold, wind, and snow that transforms our landscape into a sleeping giant and threatens to turn us mere mortals into hermits. For winter in our little part of the world is a season often dominated by the recluse as activity gives way and surrenders to dormancy. Daily life becomes a time for reflection as individuals look inward, quiet their mind and soul, and dream and plan for the days ahead when the air and water warm, and eventually purify the inevitable discontent that follows as the seemingly endless winter season drones on and refuses to release its grip.

At least that's what I've telling myself and anyone else who will listen to the soliloquy I've been blabbering the past five minutes through chattering teeth and severely chapped lips. Josie is giving me her *wrap it up* look that consists of pursed, narrow lips and a body-piercing glare it's best to avoid returning lest your eyes burn in their sockets. But I feel compelled to continue waxing poetic as I force my mind to think about anything else other than my frozen feet.

"Yes, we need to think of winter as an invitation," I said, hands on hips as I surveyed the scene in front of us. "An invitation to *crystallize* our inner thoughts and skate through winter, gliding over even the biggest challenges life may put in front of us."

1

"Suzy?"

"Yeah?"

"Shut up. It's twelve below zero, and I can't feel my legs," Josie said. "Who holds a carnival in the middle of February?"

"It's the *Winter* Carnival," I said, gliding away on my skates then circling back around her. "Take a look around. Have you ever seen anything this beautiful?"

"Is that a trick question?" she said.

"Absolutely not," I said, pointing down at the ice. "What do you see down there?"

"I see a fish," Josie said. "And I bet it's warmer than we are."

"What else do you see?"

"Water, some plants, a couple more fish. What's your point?" Josie said, glancing up at me.

"My point is that it's like looking down at an aquarium," I said.

Most years, winter arrived with a flurry of snowstorms and vicious wind that turned the shoreline into a jagged outcrop of snow and ice. But occasionally, Mother Nature was kind enough to transform miles of the River into the world's largest ice skating rink. In late January, we had a warm spell where the temperatures hit fifty during the day and hovered near freezing at night. And all of the River ice that had formed up to that point melted. On the first of February, the temperature dropped precipitously and stayed below zero for the next three weeks. And along with the freezing temperature that consistently hit minus thirty at night was the absence of snow. Now, a six-inch sheet of ice resembling glass stretched for miles up and down the shoreline of the St. Lawrence. It was only the third time I'd seen it in my lifetime and, freezing temperatures aside; it was magnificent.

A hockey puck glided past us. I looked upriver and saw a young boy waving at another who was downriver several hundred yards away. The puck finally arrived at its destination and the second boy sent it back. When the puck eventually again crossed our path, I glanced at Josie who couldn't help but smile.

"Yeah, that's pretty cool," she conceded, pushing off on the toe of one of her skates and gliding away.

A lot of people hated winter with a passion; others considered it their favorite season. Like me, Josie fell somewhere in the middle and, during the time she'd lived here, had developed strategies designed to help her cope with the cold and snow. But when her coping mechanisms failed to deliver the results she expected or pushed her outside the boundaries of her comfort zone into situations out of her control, Josie turned, in a word, cranky.

As a native of Georgia, Josie's skating as a kid had been confined to roller skates. But after several years as a local, she'd gotten good on ice skates, although she preferred to do her skating in the relative comfort of an ice skating rink surrounded by heaters and hot chocolate. But this weekend everyone was outside enjoying the expanded Winter Carnival the Town Council, led by my mother, had quickly put together to take full advantage of the see-through, six-inch sheet of glass.

I skated over to my SUV that was parked a few feet away on the ice and grabbed my binoculars. Dozens of cars, trucks, and snowmobiles filled the inner bay and, at the far end about a mile away, an ice fishing derby was in progress. At the other end of the bay, four makeshift hockey rinks had been set up, and a tournament was in progress. In between the two major organized events, people were practicing their double axels, playing broomball, drinking, and doing other assorted activities to help them take their minds off the cold.

3

I lowered my binoculars and set them down on the front seat then skated back to Josie who was practicing small jumps.

"Try putting a bit more weight on the front of your jump foot," I said, watching her struggle to get airborne. She nodded and tried another jump. "Wow. That was a good one."

"Thanks," Josie said. "I've got a good teacher."

"Incoming!"

We turned just in time to see Chef Claire barreling toward us. This winter was her first time on skates. And while she'd quickly learned the skating process and how to move forward, Chef Claire was still working on how to stop. She slammed into us, and we all collapsed in a heap on the thick ice.

"Sorry about that," Chef Claire said, climbing to her feet. "Are you guys okay?"

"Define okay," Josie said, groaning as she got up. "You need to work on learning how to put the brakes on."

"Yeah, I know," Chef Claire said, laughing. "But it's so much fun going fast on these things."

"For somebody who wasn't sure if she would be able to handle the winters, you sure seem to be okay with it," I said.

"Are you kidding? I love all of it," Chef Claire said, her eyes dancing and her cheeks flushed ruby-red. "I just came over to tell you that lunch is ready."

"Great," Josie said. "What are we having?"

"Well, I thought I'd stay with hot dishes since we're out here."

"Good call," Josie said, nodding her head vigorously.

"I'm starving," I said.

That's a major understatement. Since New Year's, I'd been working on a resolution to drop the seven pounds I'd gained since last summer. By the time Valentine's Day had rolled around, I'd made it. But it hadn't been easy saying no to a lot of Chef Claire's food. And Valentine's Day itself had caused a temporary setback when Josie and me, once again dateless, had chosen to buy two of the biggest boxes of chocolate we could find. We'd spent the evening in front of the fire in our pajamas willing to watch anything except romantic movies, sipping champagne, and working our way through an assortment of chocolates filled with cream, nougats, nuts, caramel, and other assorted surprises. But I'd shaken off that setback and refocused my efforts. Now I was down a total of ten pounds and ready to eat.

"So what's on the menu?" I said, trying to sound casual.

"Beef bourguignon, chicken vindaloo, and that tomato-basil soup you both like so much," Chef Claire said.

"Okay, you got me," I said, skating toward the back of my SUV. "What do you say, Josie?"

"Oh, no. Not the briar patch."

Chef Claire opened the back hatch of the vehicle where several warming trays were stacked. She removed a folding card table and placed it next to the car out of the wind. We all paused when we heard the roar approaching us.

"I don't believe it," I said, shaking my head.

"Man, that thing is fast," Chef Claire said.

The black snowmobile continued to speed toward us and then came to a long, skidding stop right in front of the car. My mother, dressed head to toe in a shocking pink snowmobiling suit, turned off the powerful machine, removed her pink helmet, and smiled at us as she shook her hair into place. The man sitting behind her continued to clutch her waist with both hands as he held on for dear life.

"Wentworth, as much as I love feeling your arms around me, you can let go now," my mother said. "We've stopped."

"Are you sure?" the man said as he reluctantly released his grip.

"Fear is such an unappealing trait in a man," she said.

"Well, I'm sorry, my dear," Wentworth said. "At the moment, it's all I have to offer."

"Hello, darling," my mother said, beaming at me.

"Hi, Mom," I said.

"Josie. Chef Claire," she said, climbing off the seat. "How are you ladies today?"

"We're great, Mrs. C.," Josie said. "Hi, Wentworth."

The man sitting at the back of the snowmobile gave us a small wave as he struggled to his feet, slipped and almost fell on the ice, then sat back down on the edge of the seat to remove his helmet. He looked less than pleased to be here. The wind, now gusting, blew his white hair to one side of his head. He ran his fingers through it in an attempt to put it back in place, then gave up.

"You're just in time for lunch," Chef Claire said. "Are you hungry?"

"I'll let you know as soon as my stomach leaves my throat," Wentworth said in a clipped British accent.

We'd met my mother's new boyfriend a couple of times and liked him. But he was very proper in a traditional English sort of way, and I knew my mother was doing her best to loosen him up. I doubted if an eighty-mile-an-hour snowmobile ride with a wind chill factor of minus sixty was the way to do it, but I'd learned the hard way not to argue with my mother when it came to how she handled the men in her life.

"Mom, that snowmobile is too powerful for you to handle," I said.

"Nonsense, darling," my mother said.

6

"Listen to her," Wentworth said. "Please."

Josie laughed.

"Nice snowmobile suit, Mrs. C.," Josie said.

"Thanks," she said, twirling in her boots. "Do you like it?"

"It's very…," Josie said.

"Pink," I said. "The word you're looking for is pink."

"Darling, relax," my mother said. "I'm perfectly comfortable handling this machine. And this suit makes me feel downright *sassy*."

"What does Wentworth do again?" Josie whispered.

"Lawyer?" I whispered. "No, I think he's a banker."

Josie nodded and lost interest in the conversation when she caught a whiff of the vindaloo.

"If you guys can get the folding chairs set up, I'll get everything ready," Chef Claire said.

We each grabbed a chair and arranged them around the table. Chef Claire grabbed a large tablecloth from the back of the SUV and walked to the front of the car to give herself enough room to unfold it.

"Let me just get this on the table before I serve," Chef Claire said, holding the tablecloth over her head with both hands.

"I wouldn't do that out there, Chef Claire," I said, getting up out of my chair.

"What do you mean?" Chef Claire said, flipping the tablecloth open with both hands.

The wind grabbed it and turned it into a sail.

"Uh-oh," I said, staring at Chef Claire as she began moving away from us.

We watched as the helpless Chef Claire quickly picked up speed.

"Why doesn't she just drop the tablecloth?" my mother said, staring into the distance.

7

"She loves going fast," Josie said. "I think she learned that from you, Mrs. C."

"Well, eventually she has to stop, right?" Wentworth said.

"She hasn't learned how to stop yet," I said, watching the red and white checkerboard sail flap in the breeze.

"Should we wait, or can we go ahead and start eating?" Josie said.

I stared at Josie.

"I think we should probably wait for her," I said.

"How long is it going to take her to get back?" Josie said. "I mean, we don't want it to get cold."

"Man, she's motoring," my mother said as she watched Chef Claire disappear into the distance. "Maybe I can figure out a way to hook up a sail to my snowmobile."

"Uh, let's not go there, Mom," I said, skating around the car to retrieve my binoculars.

I looked through them and watched Chef Claire race past several startled onlookers. Then she lost her balance, fell down, but continued to slide across the ice for several hundred feet. I watched her turn over on her knees laughing, then she stopped, and a look of panic appeared and remained on her face.

"I think she might be hurt," I said.

I ran to my mother's snowmobile. I sat down, started the engine, then roared toward Chef Claire. About a minute later, I came to a sliding stop next to her. She continued to stare down through the ice.

"Are you okay?" I said, skating closer to her.

"Yeah, I'm fine," she said, still staring down below the surface. "Certainly better than him."

8

I followed her eyes and then my stomach roiled when I saw the frozen body staring up at us through the ice. He was wearing a tee shirt and shorts.

Not that the dead man's seasonally-inappropriate fashion choice mattered a whit.

Chapter 2

"If you'll stay here with the snowmobile, I'll go find Jackson and Freddie. Just keep an eye on the body."

"Keep an eye on the body?" Chef Claire said, frowning at me. "Suzy, I don't think he's going to swim away."

"No, what I meant was make sure he doesn't drift off to another section of the bay," I said.

"I don't know if I can force myself to look at him," Chef Claire said, sneaking a quick peek at the body.

"Just do your best," I said. "I'll be back in a couple of minutes."

I skated off in the direction of the makeshift hockey rinks and eventually located Jackson, the Clay Bay Chief of Police, playing goalie for one of the old-timer's teams. I came to a stop on the other side of the boards and glanced at the scoreboard that showed Jackson's team on the wrong side of a 13-2 score.

"Hey, Jackson," I said.

"I'm a little busy at the moment, Suzy," he said, hunched forward and staring at the action in front of him on the ice.

"That's odd," I said, chuckling. "Given that score, I'd be surprised if you've even worked up a sweat."

"So you just stopped by to mock, right?" he said, still not turning around.

"No, I need you right now," I said, stamping my feet against the cold.

"Let me guess," he said, managing to stop a weak slapshot. "It's the goalie equipment you find irresistible."

10

"Jackson, it's minus twelve and going down fast," I snapped. "I'm really not in the mood."

"All right," he said, finally turning around when a timeout was called. "What's the problem?"

"You mean aside from your goaltending?" I said with a smirk.

"Funny."

"We just found a body," I whispered.

"We?"

"Well, actually Chef Claire found it."

"Chef Claire? Is she okay?" Jackson said, removing his goalie mask.

I'd been wrong. His face and head were plastered with sweat.

"She's fine. But you need to towel off," I said. "The last thing you need is hypothermia."

"No, the last thing I need right now is a dead body to deal with," Jackson said, wiping his brow with his jersey sleeve.

He glanced around the ice, spotted Freddie, and waved at him. Freddie, our local medical examiner, skated toward us and stopped next to me on the other side of the boards.

"Hey, Suzy," Freddie said, tugging his red and black toque down over his ears.

"Hey, Freddie," I said. "I like your toque."

"Thanks," he said, smiling at me. "Chef Claire got it for me."

Freddie paused and glanced at Jackson who chose to ignore Freddie's comment. Jackson and Freddie were fully engaged in an ongoing attempt to win the affection of Chef Claire, and their competition, while mostly friendly, occasionally had its awkward moments.

This was one of them.

"It doesn't matter," Jackson said. "I wouldn't wear a hat like that anyway."

"Whatever you say, Chief," Freddie said, shaking his head. "Enjoying the drubbing we're getting, Suzy?"

"I just got here," I said. "I need to see both of you."

"What is it?"

"Dead body," I said.

"Really?" Freddie said. "Where?"

"Over there," I said, pointing off into the distance. "He's under the ice. You two need to get over there before it starts to draw a crowd. The children will have nightmares."

"Are you sure he's dead?" Jackson said.

"Oh, yeah," I said, nodding. "I don't think the tee shirt and shorts were the right choice."

"What?" Jackson said, glancing at Freddie.

"It looks like he's been in the water for quite a while," I said.

"Okay," Jackson said, waving to another player before sitting down on the ice to remove his goalie equipment.

The other player arrived and listened to Jackson then began putting on the large pads. Freddie skated off to collect his and Jackson's belongings then joined me. We skated toward the spot where Chef Claire was huddled on the seat of the snowmobile shivering. She stood as we approached and was happy to accept hugs from both men.

I was sure her motivation at the moment was more about the search for warmth than affection, but I said nothing.

"Let's have a look," Jackson said, kneeling down and peering through the ice at the body. "Yeah, he's dead all right."

"Good work, Sherlock," Freddie said.

"Don't start," Jackson said, glaring up at him over his shoulder.

12

"I don't recognize him," Freddie said, kneeling next to Jackson. "Do you?"

"No," Jackson said. "A tee shirt and shorts? Is it possible he's been in there since summer?"

"I guess anything's possible," Freddie said. "But I would have expected to see more deterioration if he went in when the weather was still warm."

"Yeah, me too," Jackson said. "If he did go in recently, there's a pretty good chance he was snap-frozen. That would explain his relative freshness."

"Eeeww, Jackson," Chef Claire, making a face. "You're talking about the poor guy like he's a bag of peas."

"Sorry, Chef Claire," Jackson said, glancing over his shoulder.

Freddie allowed himself a small smile. Then he saw me watching him, and it disappeared.

"We'll need to cut him out," Jackson said, climbing to his feet. He removed his phone from his jacket and dialed a number. "Jimmy. It's Jackson...Yeah, I know. I gave up a dozen goals...Funny...Look, I need you to get a couple of guys and grab your chainsaws and meet me about a quarter mile upriver of the hockey tournament...I'll tell you when you get here. Thanks."

Jackson put his phone away and looked at us.

"Look, there's no reason for you two to stick around. Why don't you head home and get warm? I'll swing by later as soon as we know anything."

"Me too," Freddie said, smiling at Chef Claire.

We said our goodbyes, and I started the snowmobile as Chef Claire climbed aboard behind me. As I sped toward the rest of our group I had to marvel at the power of the machine. And while it was without a doubt too much horsepower for my mother to handle, I knew that arguing with her would only increase her determination to keep it, or perhaps even buy a bigger one. So I resigned myself to that fact and could only hope that when she fell off, as I was certain she would do at some point, she landed in a big, fluffy snowbank.

I brought the snowmobile to a stop near the running car and noticed that my mother, her boyfriend, and Josie were sitting inside the car with the heater on full blast. I sat down outside, removed my skates, and rubbed my feet which were approaching frostbite. I pulled on my thick, felt-lined boots and climbed into the driver's seat. Chef Claire hopped in the backseat next to my mother. The warm car felt wonderful, and I exhaled loudly.

"What took you guys so long?" Josie said.

"I found a dead body under the ice," Chef Claire said.

"Oh, no," Josie said, turning around in her seat to look at Chef Claire. "Is it anybody we know?"

"No, he's a stranger," I said, shaking my head.

"Well, that is certainly going to put a damper on the Carnival festivities," my mother said.

"Yeah, I imagine word will spread pretty quickly once the recovery team arrives," I said. "Jackson and Freddie are already there."

"How are they going to get him out?" Josie said.

"Chainsaws," Chef Claire said.

"Yuk," Josie said.

"Yeah, yuk is a word for it," I said. "Say, did you guys eat yet?"

"No, we were waiting for you," Josie said. "I didn't even nibble."

"Yes, dear," my mother said, reaching forward to pat Josie's arm. "You showed remarkable restraint."

"Thanks, Mrs. C.," Josie said. "Can we eat now?"

"I thought we'd head home where we can eat in front of the fire," I said.

"Works for me," Josie said. "Full speed ahead, Commander."

"Why don't you and Wentworth join us, Mom?"

"That sounds lovely, darling. Are you ready to get back on the machine, Wentworth?"

"Uh, maybe one of the ladies would enjoy the experience, my dear," he stammered. "I mean, I don't want to hog all the fun."

"You're such a baby," my mother said, laughing. "What do you say, Josie? Feel like a little ride?"

I caught Wentworth's pleading eyes in the rear view mirror and laughed. Josie chuckled and nodded.

"Sure, Mrs. C.," Josie said, climbing out of the car. "Say, how about I drive?"

"Maybe next time," my mother said, opening the back door and pulling on her hot pink leather gloves.

"Okay, Speed Racer, we'll meet you back at the house," I said.

"I certainly hope so," Josie said, climbing onto the back of the snowmobile.

Chapter 3

I had already changed my clothes, restocked the wood for the fireplace, and was sipping a Kahlua-coffee in front of the fire with Chloe, my gorgeous Australian Shepherd, and Captain, Josie's new Newfie puppy, draped across my lap when Josie stormed into the living room. My mother trailed close behind carrying her pink helmet.

"You really need to relax, Josie," my mother said, laughing.

"No, Mrs. C.," Josie said, staring at my mother in disbelief. "You need to get rid of that thing and get something safer. Like maybe a pair of snowshoes."

"What happened?" I said, laughing.

Josie shook her head in disgust but melted when she picked up Captain and held him to her chest. "How's my beautiful boy?"

"I thought you had a zest for life, Josie," my mother said, unzipping her pink snowmobile suit.

"I do," Josie said. "And the key word here is *life*. What is wrong with you? You turn into a complete maniac when you get on that thing."

My mother snorted and stepped out of her snowmobile suit revealing a head to toe black lycra bodysuit that clung tight. I had to give it to her. She looked magnificent. Wentworth seemed to agree since he flinched when he saw the bodysuit and spilled coffee on his lap.

"Easy does it, Wentworth," I said, laughing as I tossed him a napkin. "But I imagine that will be enough to get you back on the snowmobile for the ride home later."

"Yes, indeed," he said, his face flushed with embarrassment.

"So what did you do, Mom?"

"I didn't do anything," she said, making herself one of the Kahlua coffees and taking a sip. "Ah, that's good. It turns out that Josie is a big baby."

"She hit eighty on the trail that runs along the back of the high school, almost ran over a flock of geese, and then *jumped over* the street down the hill," Josie said, again giving my mother a bewildered look.

"The geese were fine," my mother said. "I blew my horn, and they flew away."

"I've got feathers in my helmet that says otherwise, Mrs. C."

"And I had to jump across the street," my mother continued. "There's no snow on the road, and I can't drive my machine across a bare road."

"When you say you jumped the road," I said, not quite believing what I was hearing. "You don't mean-"

"That's exactly what she means," Josie said. "Up the snowbank on one side doing seventy miles an hour, flying across the road, and landing on the bank on the other side."

"Really, Mom?"

"It was like a frostbitten version of Space Mountain," Josie said, kneeling down on the floor to give Captain a tummy rub. "I was terrified."

"She's just exaggerating," my mother said, sitting down next to Wentworth. "It wasn't like that at all, darling."

"Mom, you need to be careful on that thing," I said.

"Of course, darling," she said, bored with the conversation. "I'm starving."

17

On cue, Chef Claire came into the living room to announce that lunch was ready. We headed to the kitchen, filled our plates, then returned and sat eating in front of the blazing fire. I tried to stop myself at one serving of the Beef Bourginon but failed miserably. We finished with snifters of a thirty-year-old cognac that Wentworth had brought and massive slices of Boston cream pie topped with a warm chocolate-raspberry ganache that were both total knee-bucklers. I was certain the bottle of cognac cost more than my car, and I had to admit that my mother's new boyfriend certainly knew his brandies.

I was also impressed when I watched him coax my mother into having a second glass, then used that as an excuse for her not to drive the snowmobile home. Josie offered to drive them back to my mother's house with a promise that we'd bring the snowmobile back in the morning. I gave Wentworth a small knowing smile on his way out, and he winked back at me. My opinion of him went up a notch, and I hoped my mother would keep him around awhile.

When Josie returned, the three of us sprawled out to watch a movie, and I curled up with Chloe on one of the couches and dozed intermittently for the next couple of hours. Around six, Josie and I headed down to the Inn to check in with Sammy and all the dogs currently residing with us. Tripod, Sammy's three-legged Cocker Spaniel Josie and I had rescued from a puppy mill, then gave to Sammy for Christmas, greeted us when we came in the back door.

Sammy was cleaning up from the dogs' dinnertime and laughing at the reluctance several dogs were showing about going out for their evening pee.

"Are they giving you a hard time?" I said, shaking my head at various dogs who were standing in the open doorways that led outside to the two-acre play area that was now encrusted with snow and ice. They were all giving us a look that seemed to say; *you must be joking.*

"Yeah, but I can't say that I blame them," Sammy said.

"Is everything okay?" Josie said, glancing around.

"Yeah, everything's fine," Sammy said. "As soon as I can get them all outside and settled back in, I'm going to head out."

"How's Dapper doing today?" Josie said.

"He's the same. Very friendly, but he's still…what's the word?"

"Despondent," I said.

"Yeah, that's it, despondent," Sammy said.

I approached the condo where the male Dandie Dinmont resided. We'd found him along the side of the road just before winter had arrived, and he'd been with us ever since. When we discovered him, scared but in good health, he was wearing a scarf but no collar. And since the tartan scarf gave him such a distinguished look, Josie had named him Dapper and bought several scarfs for him we now had in rotation.

He now responded to his new name, but he maintained the air of despondency we attributed to his being homesick. And we had contacted every breeder of Dandie Dinmont in the country, and they had searched their records to identify if any of their clients were missing their dog. But we came up empty, so we decided to keep him. Dapper welcomed and, at times, even seemed to enjoy our company, but something was missing in his life, and his dark, sad eyes exuded melancholy and only contributed to our anxiety about not being able to do more for him.

Josie and I were somewhat familiar with the breed and knew the Dandie was from the Terrier family and originally bred in Scotland to hunt otter and badger. Dapper could have been the poster-child for the breed. He was about a foot tall, weighed around twenty pounds, and was calm and extremely intelligent. The fact that he wasn't neutered was an ongoing topic of conversation between Josie and me. Normally, we wouldn't have thought twice about neutering a male rescue, but Josie was convinced that Dapper had to be some breeder's prize possession. And since the Dandie is one of the rarest and most endangered of all purebred dogs, Josie had convinced me that we needed to hold off on his neutering. When I learned that about only a hundred puppies are born each year in the States, compared to 60,000 Golden Retrievers, I readily agreed. Neither Josie nor I would do anything that might increase the chances that this magnificent breed could become extinct.

I opened the door to Dapper's condo, and he trotted over to accept my overtures. I scratched his ears, and gently rubbed the distinctive poof of hair on top of his head. But when he dropped down in front of me and gazed up at me with his sad eyes I found myself choking back a lump in my throat.

"How are you doing, Dapper?" I said, rubbing his head.

"I was doing some research on the Dandie Dinmont," Sammy said, standing in the doorway of Dapper's condo.

"Good," Josie said, nodding. "I like to hear that. What did you find?"

"Did you know that the Dandie Dinmont is the only dog named after a fictional character?" he said.

"Yes, I did know that," Josie said. "Up until the early 1800's, they were just called Terriers. Then they got their name from Sir Walter Scott in his book, Guy Mannering, published in 1814."

"Actually," Sammy said, puffing with pride. "Scott started writing the book in 1814, but it wasn't published until early the next year. And that book also goes by the name, The Astrologer."

"Well, would you take a look at who's been studying," Josie said, laughing.

Sammy cleared his throat and began reciting from memory.

"He evolved from the Scottish Hillside, the gray mists forming his body, a bunch of lichens his topknot, crooked juniper stems his forelegs and a wet bramble his nose."

Sammy, pleased with his performance, took a small bow.

"It took me forever to understand what Scott was saying, but I think I've finally got it," Sammy said.

We both stared at him until he got embarrassed, and resumed cleaning up.

"Now he's quoting Sir Walter Scott?" Josie whispered.

"Yeah, I think we've created a monster," I whispered back.

"And I think I heard him on the phone yesterday talking with a jeweler about a ring," Josie whispered.

"No. Really?"

"Yeah. I think so," Josie said.

"Do you think he and Jill are ready for that?" I said.

Josie thought about it and then shrugged.

"We don't get a vote on that one," she said, giving Dapper a final head scratch before closing the door to his condo.

"Yeah, you're right," I said. "But they've only been dating about six months. And they're so young."

"Suzy," Josie said, her voice raising a notch. "Our job is to support, not interfere."

"I know that," I said. "Are you saying you're worried about me sticking my nose into their business and snooping around?"

"Normally, I would be," Josie said, laughing. "But not this time."

"Why not?"

"Because there's an unsolved murder you're already focused on," she said. "And you'll be far too busy obsessing over that to spend a lot of time worrying about Sammy and Jill's plans for the future."

"Maybe he just drowned," I said, then focused on something that had been bothering me all day. "But I think I saw some bruising on the body."

"See?"

"See what?"

"You just proved my point," Josie said, punching me gently on the arm. "Come on. I'll race to the last piece of Boston cream pie."

"I'll need a head start," I said.

"Not a chance," she said, dashing for the back door.

Chapter 4

By nine o'clock we were settled in for the evening in our pajamas and surrounded by snacks. Josie had opted for the lotus position and a massive sandwich on crusty bread. A pile of crumbs was rapidly building in her lap which I was doing my best to ignore. Chef Claire was sprawled in one of the overstuffed chairs and munching on a homemade granola that had sounded horrible when she first described what was in it. Now, she had to hide it from us.

As for me, I was making short work of a bowl of popcorn and wearing a thick flannel pair of pajamas with a girly-girl floral pattern my mother had gotten me for Christmas. Given the pattern, I would have never chosen them for myself, but I had to give Mom credit. They were incredibly warm and comfortable, and I loved the elastic waistband. Not that I needed it at the moment, but it was good to be prepared just in case things got out of hand again.

Chloe was sound asleep in front of the fire, and Captain slept tucked against her chest on his back with all four legs in the air. His chubby puppy tummy was on prominent display.

"Look at that," Josie said, laughing. "You sure you got a photo of that, right?"

"Yeah, we got it covered. I forced myself to stop at a dozen," I said, shaking my head at the two snoring dogs.

"You guys should swing by the restaurant tomorrow and check out all the progress," Chef Claire said, tossing a handful of granola into her mouth. "The bar has been installed, and they've got the floors sanded. It's going to look amazing when it's done."

We were in the process of renovating an old building downtown that would house our new restaurant. The three of us, along with my mother, had put together a partnership a few months ago and, around Memorial Day, *C's* would be opening. We were confident it would be a success given Chef Claire's abilities and her reputation that was rapidly spreading throughout the local area. Everything was ahead of schedule and the only major decision left to make was for Chef Claire to decide if she wanted to continue living with us at the house or whether she would move into the remodeled apartment above the restaurant. Josie and I were hoping she'd stay with us but knew that at least part of Chef Claire's decision would be based on how her increasingly confusing situation with Jackson and Freddie played out.

"That sounds good," I said. "What time should we stop by?"

"Anytime is fine," Chef Claire said. "But if you want to come by around lunch, I think it's my turn to buy."

"I'm in," Josie said, biting into the crusty sandwich.

"Now there's a surprise," I said.

"I'm really making a mess here," Josie said as she stared down at the pile of crumbs in her lap.

"That sandwich is the size of a football," I said. "Please tell me you've gained at least a pound."

"Nope," she said, shaking her head as she took another bite.

"Life is so unfair," I said.

Josie shrugged, then we all glanced toward the kitchen when we heard the quick knock followed by the sound of the door opening.

"Hey, guys," Jackson called.

"Shoes and boots stay in the kitchen," I called back.

Moments later, Jackson and Freddie entered the living room and glanced around. Chloe and Captain stirred, took a quick look around,

24

and went back to sleep. Jackson and Freddie both made a beeline for the empty chair next to Chef Claire, but Jackson managed to land first. Freddie settled for the empty couch along one wall, glanced at Chef Claire and patted the spot next to him. Chef Claire smiled at him but stayed right where she was.

"She's not a dog, Freddie," Josie said, laughing.

"Shut up," Freddie said.

"You guys want a glass of wine? Maybe a beer?" I said, getting up and handing my bowl of popcorn to Freddie.

They both decided on wine, and I served them, then resumed my position on the couch. Freddie offered me the bowl of popcorn, but I waved him off.

"That's a great pair of pajamas, Chef Claire," Freddie said.

"Thanks. I love them," Chef Claire said, smiling at Jackson.

"I got them for her," Jackson said, then looked at Chef Claire.

Freddie's face dropped at the news.

"Why aren't you wearing the tennis bracelet I got you?" Jackson said, reaching over to pat her hand.

"I was about to ask the same thing," Freddie whispered.

Josie snorted, and I did my best to stifle a laugh. Jackson and Freddie had both given Chef Claire the identical diamond bracelet for Christmas, and she was still struggling with the decision to wear both, one, or neither. Josie and I had been encouraging her to wear one and keep both suitors guessing, but Chef Claire had opted for neither at the moment.

"Well, since I'm in the middle of the restaurant renovations all day," Chef Claire said, choosing her words carefully. "I'm worried that the bracelets could get damaged. And it just seems a bit strange to wear them around the house. You know what I mean, right?"

She glanced back and forth between Jackson and Freddie and, eventually, both of them nodded.

"Sure, sure," Jackson said.

"Makes perfect sense to me," Freddie said, digging through the bowl of popcorn.

Josie leaned over closer to me.

"This is so much fun," she whispered.

"Yeah, and you wanted to watch a movie," I whispered back, grinning at Chef Claire. "So, guys, what's the news on the man under the ice?"

"Well, not a lot at the moment," Jackson said. "He didn't have any identification on him."

"Are there any missing person reports that match his description?" I said.

Jackson shook his head and took a sip of wine.

"Do you have any idea when he went into the water?" I said.

"Hard to tell right now," Freddie said. "It's going to take a couple of days to thaw him out. Right now, about the only thing I can say is that he looks like a human Popsicle. What flavor is still undetermined."

"Eeeww," Chef Claire said. "Thanks for sharing that, Freddie. Now I'm sure I'm going to have nightmares."

"If you don't mind, Freddie," Josie said. "I'm trying to eat a sandwich here."

"Yeah, I can see that bit of news really slowed you down," Freddie deadpanned.

Josie made a face at him and took another bite of roast beef.

"I thought I saw some bruising on him," I said.

"You've got a good eye, Suzy," Freddie said. "He has a big one on the left shoulder, and a couple more on his ribcage."

26

"Not to mention the big knot on the back of his head," Jackson said.

"So he *was* hit before he went into the water," I said.

"Not necessarily," Jackson said. "He could have gotten them from bouncing off the bottom." Then Jackson paused and stared at me. "Wait a minute. What are you inferring?"

"I'm not inferring anything," I said.

"Suzy," Jackson said, his voice rising in warning. "Don't go jumping to any conclusions."

"I'm not jumping anywhere," I snapped. "It just seems odd that the guy would have gotten all those bruises just from sitting in the water all that time."

"All what time?" Jackson said, not ready to let the conversation go.

"Jackson, the guy was wearing a tee shirt and shorts," I said, my voice rising. "I seriously doubt if he was recently walking around dressed like that. It hasn't been above zero in a month."

"Maybe he was a member of the Polar Bear Club," Josie said. "Those people are insane."

"You're not helping," I said to Josie.

"Disagree," she said, laughing.

"We don't have a local Polar Bear Club," I snapped.

"My aren't we snippy tonight. Well, maybe he was trying to get one started," Josie said, glaring back at me.

I didn't have a clue why I was suddenly so angry. I took a sip of wine and then patted Josie's leg.

"I'm sorry I snapped at you," I said.

"Forget it," she said. "You can't help it. Besides, when you find a dead guy under the ice in the middle of February wearing shorts and a tee shirt, you've got every right to be suspicious."

"Thank you," I said, nodding.

"But I wouldn't rule out that Polar Bear thing just yet," she said, taking another bite of her sandwich.

I waited out the laughter and then looked at Freddie.

"Did you find anything else?" I said.

"Just a couple of weird tattoos," Freddie said, reaching into his pocket.

He handed me a small stack of photos.

"The one with the eyeball surrounded by a crescent-shaped moon was on his shoulder," Freddie said. "It's a bit hard to see because of the bruising."

I glanced at the photo, then flipped to the next. I stared down at the small, yet incredibly detailed, tattoo that was on the man's left-hand index finger just below the knuckle. I handed the photo to Josie who stared down at it, then looked back up at me.

"Is that what I think it is?" Josie said.

"Yeah," I said. "It certainly is."

"What is it?" Jackson said.

"It's a tattoo of a Dandie Dinmont," I said, continuing to stare at the photo.

"A dandy what?" Freddie said.

"Dandie Dinmont," I said. "It's a dog breed."

Freddie looked at Jackson who shook his head.

"I've never heard of it," Freddie said.

"They're pretty rare," Josie said.

"Why would the guy have a dog tattoo on his finger?" Jackson said.

"Why would he be walking around in February wearing shorts and a tee shirt?" I said, beaming at Jackson.

"Okay, I'll give you that one," he said. "You might have a point. Maybe something did happen to him."

"I'm telling you, don't rule out the Polar Bear Club theory," Josie deadpanned.

"You're not helping," I said.

"Disagree."

Chapter 5

When Chef Claire had mentioned that the renovations at the restaurant were progressing nicely, she wasn't kidding. It had been a couple of weeks since Josie and I had stopped by, and the massive first floor was starting to resemble a restaurant. The kitchen was finished, and I could tell it was a huge source of pride for Chef Claire when she gave us the tour. Since there wasn't any food in sight, Josie's and my interest waned as soon as Chef Claire began waxing rhapsodic about sub-zero freezers, spacious walk-ins, and industrial chrome. After Chef Claire had a brief chat with the work crew, we headed back to my car and made the short drive to the Water's Edge, a local bar and restaurant run by our good friend Millie.

Her German shepherd, Barkley, met us at the entrance and immediately got reacquainted with his old friend Chloe. Then he spotted Captain in Josie's arms. The two dogs had never met, and Josie placed Captain on the floor, and Barkley gently placed a paw on the puppy's head before rolling over on his back. Captain took the opportunity to pounce on Barkley's chest, and they began wrestling on the floor. Chloe sat next to me, cocked her head, and watched the scene play out.

"Hey, guys," Millie said as she approached. Then she spotted Captain. "Wow. Who is this?" She bent down and picked Captain up and nuzzled him. "I'm sorry to two-time you Barkley, but I need to say hello to this beautiful boy." She held the puppy up in the air and looked Captain over, then handed him to Josie. "Newfie, right?"

"Yeah," Josie said. "He's pretty special."

"Enjoy holding him while you can," Millie said, laughing. "How big is he going to get?"

"Probably around a hundred and fifty," Josie said.

"Speaking of puppies," I said. "The shepherd litter is ready to go."

"That's great," Millie said. "Did you hear that Barkley? Your baby sister is on her way. When can I swing by to pick her out?"

"Right after Rooster decides which one he wants," I said. "We promised him first pick."

Recently we had stumbled onto an illegal puppy mill operating in the area and had ended up rescuing two litters of Labradors and another of Cocker Spaniels. And the adult German shepherd we also rescued from the mill was pregnant at the time and had delivered her litter on Christmas night. Like all the Labs and Spaniels, we knew the shepherd puppies would go fast. And Millie had raised her hand early to get her beloved Barkley a companion.

We headed for a table near the fireplace and got comfortable while Millie poured coffee. The three of us all ordered burgers and fries and started with two orders of stuffed mushrooms for the table. The deep-fried morsels soon arrived, and we dug in.

"I'm wondering something," I said, chewing one of the mushrooms.

"I think it's tarragon," Josie said, reaching for her third mushroom.

Chef Claire laughed and looked at me. I shook my head.

"What?" Josie said, glancing back and forth at us.

"I wasn't referring to the mushrooms," I said. "I'm wondering if there's a connection between the dead guy with the tattoo of the Dandie Dinmont on his finger and Dapper."

"I'm not wondering about it at all," Josie said.

31

"Why not?" I said.

"Because there has to be a connection," she said, wiping her mouth with a napkin. "What are the odds that a dog as rare as Dapper and a guy with that tattoo would just happen to show up in the same small town?"

"They're pretty long," I said, reaching for another mushroom. "And I'm wondering about something else, too."

"I think it's a dash of nutmeg," Josie deadpanned.

"Will you stop it?" I said. "I'm wondering why there's no report of a missing person."

"I was wondering the same thing," Josie said.

"And?"

"Maybe the dead guy's Canadian," Josie said.

"Now there's an idea," I said, nodding.

"You're welcome," Josie said, glancing up as Millie's approached carrying a tray. "Perfect timing."

Millie set our plates in front of us and refilled our coffees.

"I heard that you were the one who found the body under the ice, Chef Claire," Millie said.

"Yeah, that was me," Chef Claire said. "I don't recommend it."

"I bet," Millie said, shaking her head. "Have they identified who it is yet?"

"No," I said. "Jackson said nobody has a clue. They're hoping to get a picture when the guy thaws out they can use to show to people. But given the condition of the body, Jackson and Freddie aren't optimistic. Apparently, the body is a little…what was the term Freddie used?"

"Mushy," Chef Claire said.

32

"Hey, if you don't mind, I'm trying to eating my lunch," Josie said through a mouthful of fries.

"Nuclear war wouldn't ruin your appetite," I said.

Josie shrugged and picked up her burger with both hands.

"There's no missing person report that matches the guy, he didn't have any identification on him, and the only things that might help the cops figure out who he was are a couple of tattoos," I said.

"What sort of tattoos did he have?" Millie said.

"He had a weird one on his back of an eyeball and a crescent-shaped moon," I said.

"Sounds like something a member of a cult might have," Millie said, laughing as she prepared to head back to the kitchen.

"Yeah. But the strange one was the tattoo the guy had on his hand," I said.

Millie stopped in her tracks and set the empty tray down on the table next to ours.

"A tattoo on his hand?" she said.

"Yeah," I said.

"It wasn't on his index finger right below the knuckle was it?" Millie said.

Chef Claire and I stared up at her. Even Josie put her burger down.

"Yes," I said.

"A dog tattoo?" Millie said.

"How do you know that?" I said.

"Because he came in here a couple of times and sat at the bar," Millie said. "At first, I didn't even see it. But once I did, I couldn't take my eyes off it. It was incredible. He even tried to bet me a drink I couldn't identify the breed."

"When was he in here?" Josie said.

"It was definitely after Labor Day," Millie said. "I remember he was wearing shorts and a tee shirt and thought it was odd. It couldn't have been that warm."

"Do you remember anything about his clothes?" I said.

"Why are you asking me that?" Millie said, frowning.

"Because when we found him yesterday, that's what he was wearing," Chef Claire said.

"In the middle of February? What an idiot. Unless, of course, he went under the water earlier," Millie said. "But nothing specific comes to mind. Hundreds of people wearing tee shirts and shorts come in here all summer. And if it weren't for that tattoo, I wouldn't even remember him."

"Was he with anyone?" I said.

"I think he came in alone," Millie said. "But I remember he did end up drinking at the bar one night with the Baxter Brothers. I always pay close attention whenever those two cretins are in my bar."

Josie and I glanced at each other. We'd discovered that the Baxter Brothers were the ones responsible for the operation of the illegal puppy mill. They had a crime sheet longer that my arm but had disappeared right before the holidays, possibly under suspicious circumstances. I made a mental note to ask Rooster about it when he stopped by the Inn to select his puppy.

"He didn't happen to pay with a credit card, did he?" I said.

"No, I'm positive that he paid cash. He pulled a fresh hundred from a huge stack and told me to keep the change," Millie said.

"How big was the stack?" Josie said.

Millie held her thumb and index finger about an inch apart.

"That's a lot of cash to be carrying around," Josie said.

34

"That's what I thought," Millie said. "Especially when you're in the company of the Baxter Brothers."

"Do you remember anything else?" I said.

"Nah, not much," Millie said, trying to recall the memory. "But he did have a bit of an accent."

"What kind of an accent?" I said.

"I couldn't tell you," Millie said. "It sounded like he was trying to hide it, but after he had a few drinks, it started to come out. European is the closest I can come. That's about it."

"Thanks, Millie," I said. "Jackson is probably going to want to talk with you."

"Sure. Just tell him to swing by," Millie said, picking up the tray. "Look, I need to get back to the kitchen. Enjoy your lunch."

She waved goodbye and headed for the kitchen, followed closely by Barkley. I glanced under the table to check on Chloe and Captain, and they were both sound asleep. I picked up my burger and took a big bite.

"The Baxter Brothers," I said, chewing as I stared into the fireplace. "Now that's interesting."

"Maybe," Josie said, nodding.

"Do you think they could have killed him over that stack of cash?" Chef Claire said.

"That pair wouldn't have to think twice about it," I said. "When did we find Dapper on the side of the road?"

"I think it was right around Thanksgiving," Josie said. "But we've got the exact date back at the Inn."

"If Millie can pinpoint the date the guy was in here, we might be able to put some things together," I said.

"So our working theory is that the dead guy had Dapper with him. Then the Baxter Brothers beat him up and tossed him in the River?" Josie said.

"Yeah," I said. "And then the Baxter Brothers just abandoned Dapper on the side of the road."

"Well, we already know what they're capable of when it comes to dogs," Josie said, polishing off the last of her fries. "What a couple of idiots. If Dapper is the show dog we think he is, he's worth a small fortune as a stud dog."

"There's no way they would have known that," I said. "On a good day, they're lucky if they can remember their own name."

"Do you think they're still around?" Josie said.

"I don't know. I remember Jackson saying that Rooster had strongly hinted that the Baxter Brothers were no longer with us," I said.

"We need to ask him when he swings by the Inn," Josie said.

"Oh, yeah," I said, my mind racing. "This is getting interesting."

"Here we go," Josie said, shaking her head as she picked up the menu. "Is anybody up for dessert?"

"That sounds good. But I baked an apple strudel this morning," Chef Claire said. "We could just head back to the house."

"Do you ever stop cooking?" I said, staring at Chef Claire.

"Not at the moment," Chef Claire said. "We're about to open a pretty high-end restaurant. And I need constant practice to keep my skills sharp."

"Just like a musician, right?" Josie said. "You know, honing your craft and all that."

"Yeah, something like that," Chef Claire said, laughing. "Besides, I need to stay a step ahead of your ability to eat everything in sight."

"Is the strudel the one with walnuts and pecans?" Josie said.

"That's the one," Chef Claire said.

"Lead the way, maestro."

Chapter 6

Rooster Jennings was an infamous local who minded his own business, although some of the fringe elements of what his business actually involved remained murky, and he expected others to return the favor. He ran a small engine repair operation on a stretch of River shoreline he'd inherited, and, during the summer, he sold gas and sundries from his dock to unsuspecting tourists at outrageous prices. Most people avoided Rooster like the plague, which was just the way he liked it, but he and I considered each other friends. This friendship had sprung from our mutual love for dogs and started when I was still a young girl. He detested all things official and treated everyone who worked for the government or law enforcement with suspicion and a healthy dose of contempt. He lived a gruff, simple life, was worth a fortune, and, for me, was the walking definition of an enigma.

Recently, he'd helped Josie and me as we went about breaking up the illegal puppy mill we'd found operating in the area. And when he'd heard that a litter of German shepherd puppies would soon be available for adoption he'd expressed his interest in obtaining one that was loyal, would grow big, and be capable of scaring tourists on command. I'd called him last night, and he pulled his old truck into our parking area in front of the Inn just after we opened this morning at seven.

As Rooster headed up the front steps, I left my office and headed for reception. Sammy was behind the check-in desk and still working on his first cup of coffee. Upon seeing Rooster for what I assumed was the first time, he stared at the large, disheveled man wearing tattered jeans and an oil-stained sweatshirt with faded script that read; *Go ahead and ask me how my day is going. I dare you.* Sockless and wearing boots with no laces, Rooster held the front door open as he removed one of his boots and shook a small pile of snow onto the porch, put his boot back on, and let the door close behind him. He glanced around the reception area, then noticed Sammy standing behind the counter.

"Good morning," Rooster grunted. "You're Rooster Jennings, right?"

Rooster's glare landed directly on Sammy.

"Who wants to know?" he said.

"Uh, I'm Sammy. And we've been expecting you. Suzy mentioned that you were stopping by to adopt one of the German shepherd puppies."

Sammy broke eye contact with Rooster and looked around. He saw me standing near the entrance to the condo area and exhaled with relief.

"There she is," Sammy said.

"Good morning, Rooster," I said. "Cold out there this morning, huh?"

"It's February," Rooster said with a shrug.

It was hard to argue with that kind of logic, especially at seven in the morning.

"How are you doing, Suzy?" Rooster said, extending his hand.

I brushed past his hand and gave him the hug I knew he was expecting but not taking for granted.

"I'm doing good, Rooster," I said, gesturing for him to follow me. "How about we go find you a puppy?"

I stopped in front of the condo were the seven German shepherd puppies were curled up sleeping near our two Rottweilers, Rocky and

39

Bullwinkle. The puppies' mother, one of the dogs caught up in the illegal puppy mill, had been returned to its owner after the last puppy was weaned. The Rottweilers and the puppies had quickly bonded, and Rocky and Bullwinkle, always cautious around strangers, stared at Rooster as he approached the cage.

"That's a nice pair of Rottweilers," Rooster said, following me into the condo. "Are they up for adoption?"

"No, they're official members of the family. And Rocky and Bullwinkle are our nighttime security guards," I said, laughing.

"Good call," he said, chuckling as he extended his hand toward the pair of Rottweilers.

They both took several sniffs and must have decided they liked the smell of motor oil since they both allowed Rooster to pet them. Then he turned his attention to the puppies that were all waking up, excited to see a couple of visitors. Rooster sat down on the floor, and the puppies began crawling all over him.

"There are four males and three females," I said, scratching one of Rocky's ears. "And you get first pick. They've had their shots, and Josie has given all of them two big thumbs up."

"Where is Josie?" Rooster said.

I suppressed a smile. Even an old hermit like Rooster couldn't resist Josie's beauty. While Josie had been scared to death the first time she'd met him, she had quickly warmed up to the strange man and his quirky traits. Like going barefoot and wearing boots with no laces in the middle of winter.

"She's handling a new stray that was brought in last night," I said. "The poor thing got out and spent a bit too much time outside in this weather. I think Josie's almost done, but she's been up all night and might just head up to the house to get some sleep."

Rooster nodded and gave me a blank stare. I decided my explanation had fallen into his TMI category, but he said nothing. He focused on the litter, and the largest male in the litter trotted over and rubbed his head against Rooster's leg. Rooster picked him up.

"How are you, big boy?" Rooster said, gently scratching the puppy's ears.

The puppy licked Rooster's hand, and he smiled up at me.

"I think I'm picking this one," Rooster said.

"Far be it for me to correct you, Rooster," I said, laughing. "But I think it's the other way around."

"Yeah, I guess you're right," Rooster said, hopping to his feet still holding the puppy.

"You got a name picked out?" I said.

"Yup," he said. "Titan."

"Good name," I said. "Titan. I like that."

"How much do I owe you?" Rooster said, reaching into the front pocket of his tattered jeans.

"Not a thing, Rooster," I said, holding up both hands in protest.

"Don't be silly," he said, counting out ten crisp hundreds from a thick stack and handing them to me.

"A thousand dollars?" I said. "I can't take your money, Rooster."

"You can. And you will," he said. "Use it to feed a bunch of dogs."

Josie entered the condo area yawning and carrying a mug of coffee. She perked up when she saw Rooster.

"Hey, Rooster," Josie said. "I see you're taking the big guy from the litter. Great choice."

"Hi, Josie," Rooster said, doing his best not to stare at her.

"Rooster's going to name him Titan," I said.

41

"Good name," Josie said, rubbing the puppy's head.

"And Rooster just gave us a thousand dollars," I said, holding up the money.

"You didn't need to do that, Rooster," Josie said. "But thank you."

"No problem," he said. "And giving it to you is a whole lot better than giving it to the government. At least I know you two will put it to good use."

"We'll send you a reminder when Titan is about six months old, and you can bring him for his neutering," Josie said.

Rooster grimaced.

"I know it has to be done," he said, starting for the door. "But it still bothers me. I had it done to a Lab I had a long time ago, and I swear the dog never forgave me."

Josie and I both laughed as we followed Rooster. Near the door, something caught his eye, and Rooster stopped to look inside one of the condos.

"Well, I'll be," he said, glancing down at the dog who was staring up at him with sad eyes.

"That's Dapper," Josie said. "We found him along the side of the road."

"These guys are usually pretty rare," Rooster said, suddenly deep in thought.

"Are you familiar with the breed?" Josie said.

"Sure. It's a Dandie Dinmont," he said, handing Titan to me and bending down. He extended a hand through the door to Dapper's condo and stroked the dog's fur. "He's beautiful. I can't believe somebody let this guy get loose. When did you find him?"

"It was two days after Thanksgiving," Josie said, then glanced at me. "I checked the records last night."

"Hmmm," Rooster said, climbing to his feet.

"What is it?" I said, handing the puppy back to him.

"I'm just thinking," Rooster said.

I glanced at Josie, and she nodded.

"Say, Rooster," I said. "Did you hear about the guy who was found under the ice during the Carnival?"

"Suzy, when was the last time something happened in this town we didn't hear about?" he said.

"Yeah, sorry. Dumb question," I said.

"What about the body?" Rooster said.

"Well, it's just that nobody has a clue who the guy was," I said. "But we were talking with Millie at the Water's Edge yesterday, and she remembers seeing him a couple of times."

"And?" he said, switching the puppy to the other arm.

"She said that one night he was drinking at the bar with the Baxter Brothers," I said.

"Was he now? When was this?"

"She thinks it was sometime in the fall," I said.

"I see," Rooster said. "And of all the people who go and in out of her place all year, Millie just happened to remember this guy?"

"Yeah," I said, glancing at Josie before continuing. "Because of the tattoo."

Rooster stared at me until I became uncomfortable and looked away.

"Where was this tattoo?" Rooster said.

"On the index finger of his left hand right below the knuckle," I said.

"Was it a tattoo of one of those guys?" Rooster said, pointing at Dapper.

"Yes," I whispered. "How on earth did you know that?"

"Suzy, you don't want to ask me that question," Rooster said, shaking his head. "Ask a different one."

"Uh, okay," I said, glancing at Josie who shrugged. "How about, does that tattoo have any special meaning?"

"Yes, it does," he said.

"Okay. Do you know what it is?" I said.

"I know some things. Not all of it, but I know enough," he said.

"Does it have something to do with the Baxter Brothers?" I said.

"No," he said, shaking his head. "And you don't have to worry about the Baxter Brothers. Forget about them."

"But what does the tattoo mean?" I said.

"All I know is that members of a certain *club* all get them," Rooster said.

"A club?" Josie said. "Like a social club?"

"They're more like an anti-social club," Rooster said. "At least that's what I was told. But I have heard enough about these guys to tell you to stay away from them. These are some dangerous people, and if they're hanging around town, something very bad is about to go down."

"That's pretty cryptic, Rooster," I said. "Even by your standards."

"What part of stay away from these people don't you understand, Suzy?" he said, glaring at me. "I'm not joking. Do not get involved in this one. Just leave the dead guy to the cops. And you might also want to consider finding a good home in a faraway place for that little guy over there."

He glanced at Dapper, then back and forth between us until he was sure we had gotten the message. I felt a wave of fear pass through me, and I shivered. Rooster noticed and nodded.

"Good," he said. "You understand what I'm saying."

"But what do these people do?" I said.

"Suzy, as a friend, I'm warning you," Rooster said. "Stay out of this one."

"But what on earth do the Dandie Dinmont have to do with this?" I said.

"I have no idea," Rooster said. "And I don't want to know. But given how rare that breed is, and the fact that the guy you found under the ice had that specific tattoo, I'm betting there must be some connection. And if these people find out you've got that dog, you can bet they're going to show up and try to take him back."

"You keep talking about *these people*, Rooster," I said, almost pleading with him. "Who are these people?"

"I don't know, Suzy," he said. "That's what I'm trying to tell you. I've only met one of them before, and that was several years ago. And I made a promise to myself that night that I would do everything I could never to meet another one as long as I lived."

"You're scaring me, Rooster," I whispered.

"Good," he said. "Nice to see you've been paying attention. Now you two do yourself a favor and follow my advice."

I gulped and felt tears welling in the corner of my eyes.

"Just stay away from them, and you'll both be fine," Rooster said. "I need to run. Thanks again for the puppy. You guys are the best."

I gave him a small wave and watched him head for the door. Then he stopped and turned around.

"Oh, one more thing," Rooster said.

45

"Yeah," I said, exhaling loudly.

"If you two decide you can't help yourself and feel the need to stick your nose where it doesn't belong, call me before you do something really stupid."

"You mean like getting involved with those people?" Josie said.

Rooster nodded and smiled at Josie before looking at me.

"Do yourself a favor and listen to her, Suzy."

"If she does, it'll be a first," Josie said.

"That's what I'm afraid of," Rooster said.

He exited and left us standing in the middle of the condo area speechless.

And as I'm sure you know by this point, that's pretty hard to do.

Chapter 7

After Rooster had left with his new puppy, Josie and I headed to my office to catch up on some paperwork we'd been putting off. We settled in and quickly knocked off all the paperwork, reordered dog food and Josie's vet supplies for the upcoming month, then reviewed our financial statements. We always operated at a small loss during the slower winter months, and this year was no different. But the total amount was small and barely got our attention. I leaned back in my chair and put my feet up as Josie grabbed the candy dish from the desk and headed for the couch. She stopped when she heard the soft scratching coming from the other side of the door. She opened it, and Chloe and Captain trotted into the office.

I took my feet off the desk as Chloe approached and she hopped up into my lap. I groaned when she landed. She was getting bigger by the day and soon would be full grown. I tried to remind her on a regular basis that she no longer fit the description of a lap dog, but she continued to ignore me. I stroked her head as she got comfortable and she closed her eyes. Captain hopped up onto the couch with Josie and stretched out on her lap. Josie petted him with one hand as she expertly opened and tossed back bite-sized Snickers with the other.

"No, Captain," Josie said, firmly. "You can just forget it. No chocolate for you."

"Can you think of anything else we need to do?" Josie said.

"You mean apart from thinking about what Rooster said?"

"Stop thinking about it," Josie said. "He scared me half to death."

"What kind of people do you think they are?" I said, slowly rocking in my chair. "And what sort of things are they doing?"

"You're thinking about it," Josie said.

"I can't help it," I said.

"Yeah, I can't either," she said. "Why would they pick them as their breed?"

"The only thing I can think of is because the Dandie Dinmont is pretty rare. You know, they're kind of unique. Maybe that's how they think of the members of their club."

"That's a pretty good insight," Josie said.

"Thanks. I have my moments."

"But why the tattoo?" she said.

"I guess it's an easy way to identify other club members without being obvious about it," I said.

Wow. Where did that come from? My sub-conscious was wide awake and working early this morning.

"That's good," Josie said, gently sliding out from underneath the sleeping Captain to sit up on the couch. Then she walked over to the desk and stuck her hand out.

"Shake my hand," Josie said.

"What?" I said, staring at her.

"Shake my hand," she repeated.

"Wash my car," I deadpanned.

Josie snorted but continued to hold her hand in front of me.

"No, you idiot," she said, laughing. "I'm not joking. Shake my hand."

I shook my head but accepted the handshake. Josie grabbed my hand and refused to let go.

"What do you see?" she said, nodding at our grasped hands.

48

"Uh, two women with way too much time on their hands?"

"Look at my finger. The index finger," she said.

I nodded when her reference finally registered. Josie released her grip and reached for the candy bowl.

"If you had that tattoo, I'd be able to see it right away," I said. "Well done. You're good."

"And if anybody outside the club happened to notice the tattoo, it would be nothing more than a casual topic of conversation," Josie said.

"But to another member of the club, it could mean everything," I said.

"Yeah, it certainly could."

"Huh," I grunted. "So what does all that tell us?"

"Not much," Josie said, glancing at her watch. "Hey, it's almost time for lunch."

"That's right," I said. "Chef Claire said she had a surprise for us today."

"She's so amazing," Josie said. "It's kind of like living with Santa Claus."

"Yeah, and if I keep eating the way I do, I going to end up looking just like Santa."

"Oh, stop it. You look great. And you just lost ten pounds."

"Yeah," I said. "But I'm worried that if I turn around, I'm going to find it."

Josie snorted, then gently punched me in the arm.

"You know, Suzy, it takes a woman of great strength and self-confidence to make a joke about her own butt," Josie said, laughing.

"You've got a good point there," I said, grinning. "Have I got time to call Jackson before we head up to the house?"

"No need for that," Josie said, collecting Captain in her arms and giving him a hug. "Chef Claire invited him and Freddie to lunch."

"I wonder what the surprise is," I said.

I waited for Chloe to hop down before getting up out of my chair.

"I bet it has something to do with the box that was delivered yesterday," Josie said, heading for the door, still carrying Captain. "I didn't get a look at what was in it."

"Yeah, she was very secretive about it," I said.

We fought a strong headwind as we headed up the path that led to the house, taking our time going over a few snow-packed areas that had turned icy. I made a mental note to remind the kid who did our shoveling to take care of them and climbed the steps that led to the verandah. We followed both dogs inside and discovered that Chef Claire had turned the kitchen into what looked like a science experiment.

"Oh, good, you're right on time," Chef Claire said. "Freddie and Jackson are in the living room. Why don't you guys keep them company while I finish things up here? Josie, get out of there."

Josie, caught red-handed, removed her finger from a bowl of batter and looked sheepishly at Chef Claire. Then she licked her finger and nodded approvingly.

"Sorry," Josie said, then pointed at a flat metal piece of kitchen equipment. "Is that what I think it is?"

"Maybe," Chef Claire said. "What do you think it is?"

"Call me crazy," Josie said. "But it looks like the biggest waffle maker I've ever seen."

"Good guess," Chef Claire said. "Now get your hand out of there and get out of the kitchen."

"You're making waffles?" I said.

"Maybe," Chef Claire said. "I'm testing out a few new items I'm thinking about putting on the menu at the restaurant. Consider yourselves my guinea pigs."

"Oh, no," Josie said. "Not the briar patch."

"Out," Chef Claire said.

Laughing, we headed for the living room and found Jackson and Freddie chatting with each other. While there were no signs of open hostility between them, there was obvious tension in the room.

"Hey guys," Josie said, sitting down on one of the couches next to Freddie. "Any idea what she's making for lunch?"

"Not a clue," Freddie said.

Jackson shook his head and stared into the roaring fire. I made another mental note to order yet another cord of wood. It was below zero again, and we were going through firewood at a record pace.

"We had an interesting chat with Rooster this morning," I said to Jackson.

"Every conversation with Rooster is interesting," he said.

I gave him a quick recap, and he listened closely. When I finished, I sat back on the couch and pulled my legs under me in a quasi-lotus position.

I congratulated myself. Before I'd dropped those ten pounds, I would have never been able to pull it off.

"So we might be dealing with some kind of cult?" Jackson said.

"Who knows?" I said, shrugging. "But Rooster was adamant about us staying out of it."

"Good advice," Jackson said. "Are you going to take it?"

"Sure, Jackson," I said. "You know me. I'm always willing to listen to good advice."

He shook his head at me, but before he could respond, Chef Claire called us into the dining room. We sat down and looked around the table. Three covered silver serving platters were laid out on the end of the table in front of Chef Claire. Josie was sitting to her immediate right and reached for the cover of one of the platters. Chef Claire smacked Josie's hand with a wooden spoon.

"Ow," Josie said, shaking her hand. "That hurt."

"Just hold your horses," Chef Claire said, laughing.

"My mother used to do that to me all the time," Josie said.

"Good," Chef Claire said. "Okay, I know this might come across as a little weird, but I wanted to get your reaction to these dishes without you having any advance knowledge about them. I think that what I call the Oohs and Ahh factor is very important for any restaurant."

She paused to look around the table. We all nodded that we understood.

"I'll be Ooh," I deadpanned.

"And I'll be Ahh," Josie said.

"I've been thinking about different things that might get people's attention at the restaurant," Chef Claire said, ignoring us. "We know that we've got all the usual suspects well covered on the menu, but I've been thinking about additional items we might be able to include, or use as specials from time to time."

"Are we here to eat or just talk?" Josie said, glancing around at the covered platters.

"Okay, good point," Chef Claire said. "This first dish is one I'm thinking about adding to the lunch menu."

She removed the lid from one of the platters, and we all stared down at the familiar, yet somehow unknown, object.

"A double-decker waffle?" Josie said, frowning.

"At first glance, you might think so," Chef Claire said, smiling. "But let me show you."

She removed one of the objects and placed it on Josie's plate. Again, she swatted Josie's hand.

"You're worse than a little kid," Chef Claire said.

"Then stop teasing me," Josie said, staring down at her plate.

Chef Claire removed the top waffle and looked up at us.

"I'd like to introduce *The Josie*," Chef Claire said.

"You named a sandwich after me?" Josie murmured.

"I did," Chef Claire said. "It's my take on what happens when you combine a BLT with a waffle."

"I love both of those," Josie whispered.

"Yes, I know," Chef Claire said, grinning. "Hence the name. Underneath the lettuce and tomato, you'll find an over easy fried egg sitting on top of four slices of bacon. Instead of bread, I substituted a cheddar and manchego cheese waffle I cut in half. And instead of mayo or maple syrup, I use an apple butter."

Chef Claire put the top waffle back on Josie's sandwich and gestured for her to take a bite. Josie cut a large piece and slowly chewed it, then set her knife and fork down and wiped her mouth.

"Well?" Chef Claire said.

"I think I'm going to cry," Josie said.

The rest of us started working on our sandwiches and, apart from the various murmurs and sound of silverware tapping our plates, we ate in silence. Chef Claire beamed as she watched our expressions.

"This is unbelievable," Freddie finally managed.

"Thanks," Chef Claire said. "What do you think, Jackson?"

"I think I'm in love," Jackson said, then he stopped, and his face turned bright red. "I mean, I love the sandwich. Not you. I mean, I wasn't referring to you." Then he shook his head. "Forget it."

"Smooth," Josie said.

"What do you think, Suzy?" Chef Claire, doing her best to ignore Jackson's outburst.

"It's a total knee-buckler," I said, dipping a piece of waffle in a small pile of egg yolk that had collected on my plate. "How on earth did you come up with this one?"

"You solve your mysteries," Chef Claire said, laughing. "I solve mine. It was just the answer I came up with to a simple what-if question. Let's move on to the next dish, shall we?"

"Sounds great," Josie said, then leaned close to Jackson. "Try not to propose," she whispered.

Everyone laughed, and Jackson's face again flushed with embarrassment.

"I think that this one could work on both the lunch and dinner menu, but I'm leaning toward making it a special. Maybe a once a week kind of thing."

She removed the top of the next serving platter, and we saw a stack of waffles stacked next to a large pile of fried chicken.

"Chicken and waffles?" Josie said. "Oh, my goodness."

"Yeah," Chef Claire said. "I figured that with you being from Georgia, this one would get your attention."

Chef Claire filled our plates and passed them around. Then she started a gravy boat of syrup around the table.

"It's a bacon-jalapeno-rosemary waffle. I stepped on the maple syrup with red peppercorns, a splash of cognac, and some cinnamon and nutmeg. Enjoy."

Another round of silence filled the room as we worked our way through the dish. After three bites, I stared at Josie who shook her head at me in wonder.

"Chef Claire," I said, marveling at the dish. "You are simply amazing."

"Thanks, Suzy. You're awfully quiet, Freddie," Chef Claire said.

"I think I'm in shock," he said, laughing. "This is incredible."

"Jackson?" Chef Claire said.

"Shhh," Josie said, laughing. "Don't bother him. He's making plans. What do you think, Jackson? Maybe a June wedding?"

"Josie?" Jackson said.

"Yes, Jackson?"

"Shut up."

"Okay, we have one more dish," Chef Claire said. "And I'm going to apologize right up front to you, Suzy."

"What on earth do you have to apologize for?" I said, frowning.

"This," Chef Claire said as she removed the lid on the final platter. "A lobster-crab waffle."

I stared at the objects that looked exactly like the two waffles I'd just eaten. And despite my ongoing, and well-known, dislike for all food that came from the sea, I found myself being drawn in by the aroma coming off the platter.

"Are you kidding me?" Josie said.

"No," Chef Claire said, obviously very proud of the dish. "Instead of doing them on the stovetop or in the oven, I started experimenting with an old waffle iron I found in the kitchen. I thought the waffle iron might give them an interesting texture. You know, give them some extra crispy bits. I think people are going to love this one as an appetizer."

"Wow," Jackson said as he took his first bite. "What's the sauce?"

"It's a lemon-tarragon aioli," Chef Claire said. "With a healthy splash of champagne. Suzy, I know you won't eat this one, but there are more chicken and waffles in the kitchen if you're still hungry."

"No," I said, continuing to stare at the platter. "I think I might just try a little bite."

Josie stared at me, then glanced at Chef Claire. Inexplicably drawn to the lobster and crab waffle, I cut a small corner and put it in my mouth. I closed my eyes and chewed slowly. A burst of flavor flooded through me and I sighed. Then I took a much larger second bite.

"Oh, my goodness," I said, looking at Chef Claire. "How could I have been so wrong?"

"You like it?" Josie said.

"I love it," I said, digging in again.

"Hah!" Chef Claire exclaimed.

"I can't believe it," Josie said.

"What?" I said, glancing back and forth at them between bites.

"I bet her that I could get you eating seafood before the restaurant opened," Chef Claire said, smirking at Josie. "Pay up."

"Unbelievable," Josie said, digging into her scrubs and pulling out her wallet. She tossed a hundred dollar bill to Chef Claire. "I would have never believed it if I hadn't seen it with my own eyes."

"Me either," I said, staring down at my empty plate.

Chapter 8

Each year, my mother threw her *Good Riddance to February* party that had become something of a local tradition. She held the party at her house, a seven-bedroom, six-thousand square foot Victorian in the center of town she and my dad had bought years ago soon after they were married. And since it was the house I'd grown up in, a flood of memories washed over me every time I visited. It was way too much house for her and cost a fortune to heat. But the house was her last tangible, physical link to my dad who had passed way too early, several years ago.

She would never come right out and say it, but I knew she kept the house for two reasons. The first was as a tribute to him. The other arose from a fear she had that selling the house would somehow damage, perhaps even destroy, parts of the life she had shared with him. Unwilling to take the risk of fading memories, she went the other way with the house and continued to work on it. Five years ago, my mother had a new kitchen installed that had made Chef Claire envious the first time she saw it. The year after that, my mother had closely supervised - some might call it terrorized - a work crew responsible for expanding and remodeling her master suite. This year's project had been a makeover of the massive basement that stretched the length of the house.

But through all the years of remodels and expansion, my childhood bedroom remained untouched. And one time when I'd jokingly called my mother *overly sentimental*, she'd teared up when explaining that she could never do anything that might damage that particular set of family memories. I'd bawled like a baby and made a silent vow to never broach the subject again.

She greeted us at the door wearing designer jeans and a purple cashmere sweater she'd bought during a recent shopping trip I'd accompanied her on to Montreal. I'd almost fainted when I saw the price tag, but it looked amazing on her.

"Hello, darling. You're getting too skinny," she said, hugging me. "Josie, you look incredible."

"Thanks, Mrs. C.," Josie said. "That's a beautiful sweater."

"Thank you," she said, glancing down at it. "I shouldn't have done it, but Suzy just had to talk me into buying it."

"Right, Mom," I said, shaking my head.

In the store, my mother had pretty much elbowed every other shopper within ten feet out of the way when she'd spotted the sweater and made a beeline for it.

"Chef Claire," my mother said, giving her a hug. "Welcome. I know you're going to enjoy the food this evening."

"I'm sure I will, Mrs. C.," Chef Claire waving to Freddie who was standing in the great room off to our right chatting with a large group of people.

"I wish I could have used you," my mother whispered. "But I had already signed the catering contract and couldn't get out of it."

"Believe me, it's not a problem," Chef Claire said. "I'm looking forward to a night off."

"But next year I'm using you," my mother said. "And that fact isn't even up for debate."

Chef Claire, knowing my mother wasn't kidding, simply smiled and nodded.

"Where's Wentworth?" I said, glancing around.

"He'll be out soon. He's in my office talking with some of his colleagues," my mother said. "The world of high finance never sleeps, right?"

"Sure, sure," I said, giving her my best sage nod.

Josie snorted. I ignored her.

"So, Chef Claire," my mother said. "Have you made up your mind yet about Freddie and Jackson?"

"Geez, Mom," I said, blanching.

"Oh, I'm sorry," my mother said. "I didn't think it was some big secret."

"It's okay," Chef Claire said. "No, Mrs. C. I'm still struggling with it."

"You know, you might want to use the same approach I do when I'm trying to decide which new car to get," my mother said.

"This should be good," Josie whispered.

"What's that, Mom?" I deadpanned. "Take both of them for an extended test drive?"

"Funny, darling," she said, scowling at me. "What I do is sit in the front seat, close all the windows and turn on some soothing jazz. Then I just relax and let things wash over me. Soon, I have a good picture of how the car is going to make me feel."

"You're joking, right, Mom?"

"I never joke about men or cars, darling."

Chef Claire laughed.

"What do you suggest I do if both of them make me feel pretty much the same way?" Chef Claire said.

"Then you should count your blessings, my dear," my mother said, smiling and giving Chef Claire's hand a quick squeeze. "And if that's the case, take your time and enjoy the ride."

59

"My mother, the relationship guru," I said. "So, tell us, Mom. Do you think Wentworth is a keeper?"

"No, I'm afraid that Wentworth will eventually end up in the catch and release category, darling."

"I thought you liked him," I said, surprised by the news.

"Oh, I do. Very much," she said, glancing over her shoulder to make sure she was out of earshot of the other partygoers. "But there's something about him that bothers me."

"Maybe it's because he doesn't want to die an early death on a snowmobile," Josie said.

"Really, Josie?" my mother said, staring at her. "You need to let that go."

"Disagree."

"So what's bothering you?" I said.

"I'm not sure," she said. "And that's what is bothering me. There's just something a bit out of kilter with him."

"Are you sure you just aren't comparing him to Dad?"

"I stopped doing that years ago, darling," she said, patting my arm. "If I compared the men I go out with to your father, I'd be sitting around the house every night and never date. Just like you."

"Oh, good one, Mrs. C.," Josie said, laughing.

"You're one to talk," I said, glaring at Josie before turning back to my mother. "And for your information, Mom, I've been on three dates this winter."

"Yes, and I was the one who set all of them up," my mother said. "And that reminds me. One of Wentworth's colleagues who's here tonight is perfect for you."

"Ah, geez, Mom. A finance guy?" I said, scrunching my face into a scowl. "I don't think so."

60

"That's only his day job, darling. He's an animal lover, breeds horses, and loves good food and wine. He's wonderful. And apart from that ridiculous tattoo, I can't think of a single thing wrong with him."

I glanced at Josie who'd gone on point at the mention of the tattoo. I looked back at my mother and nodded.

"Okay, Mom. I'd love to meet him."

"Wonderful, darling," my mother said. "Let me go see if I can find him. In the meantime, why don't the three of you mingle? Maybe grab a cocktail and check out the buffet table."

"What a good idea," Josie said.

Chef Claire and I smiled at Josie, then followed her as she worked her way through the crowd toward the food. On the way, I stopped to say hello to several people, and by the time I'd gotten to the buffet table, Josie was already halfway through her first plate.

"Try the stuffed mushrooms," Josie said, pointing at one of the serving trays. "They're fabulous."

"Good evening, ladies."

The three of us turned around and saw Jackson beaming at Chef Claire.

"Hey, Jackson," I said.

"Great party," he said. "Your mom always does such a nice job with it. I was about to tell her that, but she just blew right past me. Is she okay?"

"She's fine," I said. "She's just looking for somebody."

"The new love of Suzy's life," Josie said.

"Shut up," I said.

"Speaking of the love of your life," Jackson said. "Can I have a word with you, Chef Claire?"

"Uh, sure," Chef Claire said, caught off guard and on edge.

"I'd like to talk in private if that's okay with you," Jackson said.

"Okay," Chef Claire said, looking around the crowded room. "That might be a bit tough to pull off."

"Why don't you go upstairs to my old room?" I said. "Nobody will disturb you up there."

"Great idea," Jackson said. "C'mon, I'll lead the way."

He grabbed Chef Claire's hand, and she glanced back at us before following Jackson across the room then up the stairs.

"Hey, Jackson," Josie deadpanned. "Remember. One foot on the floor at all times."

"You're terrible," I said, laughing. "Uh-oh, here comes Freddie."

We watched our local medical examiner approach. He obviously wasn't pleased with what he'd just witnessed.

"Good evening, Freddie," Josie said. "Why the long face?"

"Where are they going?" he said, nodding at the stairs.

"I think they said something about lying down for a while," Josie said. "Wasn't that it, Suzy?"

"Yeah, I think I heard the word *horizontal* mentioned at some point in the conversation," I deadpanned.

"You two are really funny," Freddie snapped. "You might want to try and help me out."

"Help you out with what?" I said.

"Her," he said, staring at the stairs.

"Us? You want relationship advice from us?" Josie said. "I haven't been on a date in six months, and this one never goes out unless her mother sets one up."

"Well, whose fault is that?" Freddie said.

"I don't think it's anybody's fault, Freddie," I said.

"You're too picky," he said. "Both of you."

"I thought we were talking about your problems," Josie said.

"Yeah," Freddie said, pleased with himself. "That was pretty good the way I turned it around, wasn't it?"

"Don't make a habit of it," Josie said, laughing.

"I need another drink," Freddie said. "Can I get you guys something?"

We both declined and Freddie started to make his way toward the bar that had been set up along one wall. Josie selected another mushroom from her small pile, then something caught her eye, and she put her plate of food down. Before I could come up with a joke about how rare an occurrence that was, she exhaled loudly.

"Whoa."

"What is it?" I said, following her gaze. "Wow."

We watched my mother work her way across the room gently pulling the arm of the man walking next to her. He was smiling as he listened to her incessant chatter even as he continued to take in what was happening around him. I put him in his mid-thirties, around six-feet tall, toned, and drop dead gorgeous.

"Suzy?" Josie said.

"What?"

"If you don't want him, let me know," Josie said, unable to take her eyes off him.

"Sorry, but I don't like your chances," I said.

My mother stopped in front of us, and I forced myself to look at her.

"Darling, I'd like you to meet William Wild," she said.

"Please, just call me Bill," the man said, smiling at me. "You must be Suzy."

"Nice to meet you, Bill," I finally managed to get out.

"I've heard so many good things about you from your mother," Bill said.

"I wouldn't put too much stock in what she says. She's a drinker."

"Funny, darling."

Bill chuckled at my joke then looked at Josie. He was obviously impressed by what he saw and nodded his head at her once.

"And you must be, Josie," he said, giving her a wide smile.

"It's nice to meet you, Bill," Josie said, extending her hand.

He returned the handshake, and we both saw the tattoo at the same time. I glanced at Josie and she gave me the slightest shake of her head to let it go. Then Bill did something that rarely happened when Josie and I were standing next to each other. He looked back at me and didn't take his eyes off me for several seconds. I felt a lump in my throat and swallowed hard. My mother noticed my flushed face and beamed at me.

"I just knew the two of you would hit it off," she said. "Now if you'll excuse me, there's someone who's dying to meet Josie. Follow me, dear."

I didn't even see them leave.

Chapter 9

The gorgeous man named William Wild turned out to be from a small town in Pennsylvania, but had gone to college in Philadelphia and graduated from Wharton where he'd managed to find the time to play rugby and volunteer for various charities around the city. He did post-graduate work in England and spent a few years working in London before returning to the States and setting up shop in New York working either for Wentworth. I wasn't clear on some of the details because I'd drifted off momentarily fantasizing about long walks in the English countryside with him by my side.

By the time we'd finished sharing our bios and life highlights, I was inching closer to him on the couch and very much intrigued.

Our conversation shifted from us to animals, and Bill seemed to be an expert about many of the problems and challenges animals faced around the planet. He explained that while he'd grown up hunting and fishing, he'd quit hunting several years ago and, that while he still loved to fish, he was a committed devotee of catch and release. When I joked about how I hoped that his catch and release approach was reserved for fish and not women, he laughed hard. I inched even closer, and he casually placed a hand on my knee. He gently squeezed my leg, and I waited for his hand to begin its inevitable trek north. But the hand remained in its original landing spot and, as we chatted, he managed to express genuine desire and remain a gentleman; a type of man that on many days seems destined for the endangered species list.

He spent a few minutes trying to explain what he did for a living, using a variety of financial terms that always gave me a headache. Then he realized I was bored and clueless, and, in an obvious attempt to avoid making me feel like an idiot, he seamlessly steered the conversation back to our mutual love for dogs.

Now I was dreaming about summer days with him on the River where we could head north or go in whatever direction we wanted.

When he mentioned that his biggest goal was to leave the world of corporate finance, settle down, and spend the rest of his life raising a family in a small town with four distinct seasons, I was toast.

Stick a fork in me. I was done.

But then I caught another glimpse of the elaborate Dandie Dinmont tattoo on his index finger, and I forced myself to apply the brakes. I gently grabbed his hand and examined it.

"That's an interesting tattoo," I said. "It's very detailed."

"Thanks," he said, laughing. "It's a funny story."

"Oh, please, do tell."

"One year I was in Mexico with some buddies during spring break, and after a night of *way too much* tequila, we all decided to get tattoos," he said.

I felt my stomach begin to drop.

"And we went to this guy who has a reputation for being one of the best tattoo artists around. I mean this guy is a legend. Even though I was hammered, I was still scared to death. And after I watched my buddy get an enormous tattoo of an eagle on his back, I decided to go small. When I saw this dog design in his book, I went with it."

Bill held up his finger and glanced at the tattoo.

"At first, I wasn't sure I liked it. But I have to admit, it's quite the conversation starter," he said, placing his hand back on my knee.

"The Dandie Dinmont," I said.

"Yeah," he said, "I think that's what it's called." Then he beamed at me. "But you're the expert, right?"

"Right," I said, forcing a smile. "Look, I just remembered I forgot to tell Josie something. I'll be right back."

"And I'll be right here," he said, patting the spot on the couch where I'd been sitting.

I found Josie in the kitchen debating the pros and cons of fried versus steamed dumplings with the catering crew. Judging from the stack of small plates in front of her, it appeared the debate included a rather extensive taste test. She glanced up when she saw the expression on my face and excused herself.

"Are you okay?" Josie said, following me to a corner of the kitchen.

"I was. Actually, I was doing great," I said, shaking my head. "And then he did something stupid."

"What? Did he get drunk and start making obscene comments?"

"No, he seems completely sober," I said.

"Did he try to get you horizontal on the couch?"

"Of course not," I said, frowning at her.

"Try to kiss you in public?" she said, swallowing the vestiges of her last dumpling.

"No."

"Put his hands where they didn't belong?"

"No, I was very happy with where his hands were," I said.

"Okay, I'm out of guesses. What was it?"

"He lied to me," I whispered.

"Geez," she said, putting an arm around my shoulder. "I hate when they do that."

"Yeah, me too."

"Was it about the tattoo?" she said, glancing over at Bill who was sitting quietly on the couch and nodding his head to the music.

"It sure was. He says he got it on spring break in Mexico," I said.

"I guess it's a possibility, right?" Josie said, frowning.

"No, it wasn't that it couldn't have happened the way he said it did," I said, shaking my head. "But you know the feeling you get in your gut when you first realize somebody is lying to you?"

"Yes, I do," Josie said. "And you got it?"

"I still have it," I said. "He was lying through his teeth."

"Man, you can't catch a break," Josie said. "Other than that, how did it go?"

"If I hadn't caught him in a lie, by now I'd probably be over there picking out china patterns and deciding where to register," I said, laughing.

"He is gorgeous," Josie said, then gave me a coy smile. "Well, there's always the catch and release program."

"Continue seeing someone who lies to you the first time you meet them?" I said.

"Isn't that the time most people do a lot of their lying?" Josie said. "You know, get it out there early before the facts can catch up with you."

"You're not helping," I said, laughing.

"Disagree."

"Sorry, but liars are number one on the list of creatures to avoid," I said.

"He didn't lie to me," Josie said, sneaking another glance at the couch.

"What?"

"I'm joking," she said. "But it's too bad. What a waste."

"Yeah, I know," I said. "What do you think I should do?"

"You just said it," Josie said. "Walk away. No harm, no foul."

"But what if he is somehow involved with the guy we found under the ice? Or connected with Dapper?"

"Well, there is that," Josie said. "It's too much of a coincidence for those two tattoos not to be connected in some way."

"And remember what Rooster said about how dangerous these people are?"

"Yeah, and Rooster doesn't scare easily," she said. "It sure would help if we knew a bit more about *these people*."

"So you're saying I should go out with him and see what I can find out?" I said.

Josie snorted.

Sometimes it bothered me when she did it. Other times it didn't. Since I knew where the conversation was heading, this time definitely made me cranky.

"It's funny, but I don't remember telling you to date the guy," Josie said.

"You *inferred* it," I said.

"Okay, Sherlock. Have it your way," she said, laughing. "Go ahead and go out with him. What's the worst thing that could happen?"

"I can think of a lot of different situations that could happen," I said.

"Are you wearing clothes in any of them?" Josie said.

"Maybe a couple," I said.

Then we both laughed loud enough to draw looks from several people standing nearby, including my mother who approached with Wentworth in tow.

"What did we miss, darling?"

"Oh, it's nothing, Mom," I said, giving Wentworth a small wave. "We were just chatting."

"I see," my mother said. "How's it going with Bill?"

"Actually, all things considered, not too bad," I said, unwilling to have the conversation with her at the moment.

"I'm glad to hear that," she said. "I'll have to organize another, more intimate, get together."

"That's okay, Mom. I'm perfectly capable of organizing my own intimate get-togethers."

Josie snorted again, and as I replayed my comment in my head, I felt my face flush with embarrassment.

"I'm so glad to hear that, darling," my mother said, flashing Josie a smile. "I was beginning to worry."

"Please, Mom. Don't start."

I turned to Josie.

"We should probably get going," I said.

"Yeah, it's getting late, and I have a surgery scheduled for eight-thirty," Josie said.

She didn't, but I appreciated her support in cutting off my mother's protests before she could even get started. I was about to start pondering the value of the situational lie and its proper use when another thought forced its way to the front of the line.

"Have you seen Chef Claire?" I said.

"No, I haven't," Josie said. "Not since earlier."

"How about you, Mom?"

"No, the only time I saw her all night was when you arrived," my mother said.

"Wow," I said. "I wonder if they're still up there."

"Up where, darling? And who are we talking about?"

"Uh, my room," I said. "Chef Claire and Jackson went up there to talk. But that was a long time ago."

"How about that, darling? There's a man in your bedroom," my mother said, her eyes dancing. "And yet, you're down here."

"Mom, please. Give it a rest."

"I thought it was funny, Mrs. C.," Josie said.

"Thank you, Josie. I'm glad someone appreciates my whimsical sense of humor," my mother said.

I gave up and looked at Wentworth.

"She's all yours, Wentworth," I said.

"I certainly hope you're right about that," he said, wrapping an arm around my mother's waist.

"Are you kidding?" I said. "The way she talks about you, I doubt you could get away if you tried."

"We do make a wonderful couple, don't we?" he said, giving my mother a kiss on the cheek. "Isn't that right, Snuggles?"

"Yes, Wentworth," my mother said, blushing. "We're fabulous."

"Snuggles?" I said, my eyes widening. "What a cute pet name."

I returned the cold stare my mother was giving me, then flashed her a small smile. She eventually nodded, and we silently declared a truce.

"If I see Chef Claire," my mother said. "I'll let her know you've gone home."

"Thanks, Snuggles."

I hugged her then headed for the couch to say goodbye to Bill. I exchanged phone numbers with him, returned the warm hug he gave me, then Josie and I bundled up and headed for the car. I turned the heater on full blast, and we drove in silence until I glanced over at her.

"How about you? Did you meet anybody interesting tonight?"

71

"I thought the head caterer was kinda cute, but that could have just been the mushroom effect," Josie said.

"The mushroom effect?"

"Yeah," she said. "Anybody who can work that kind of magic on fungi must be worth a second look, right?"

"I'm not even going to try arguing with that kind of logic," I said, laughing.

"Good. I'm too tired to argue," she said. "Do you think Chef Claire and Jackson...got busy up there?"

"I guess it's possible," I said.

"Two people hooking up in your childhood bedroom? That would weird me out. How does it make you feel?"

"I'd say I'm ambivalent," I said. "It's not a big deal."

"Really?"

"Yeah, when in Rome and all that, right? And if they can get past the Sleeping Beauty sheets and pillowcases, more power to them," I said, laughing.

"You're joking."

"No, memories die hard for my Mom," I said. "Despite her protests about my lack of a love life, in her mind, I'll always be eight."

We pulled into the driveway, exited the car and heard the sound of barking coming from the Inn.

"That's odd," I said, walking quickly toward the back door that opened onto the condo area.

"It sounds like Rocky and Bullwinkle," Josie said, following closely.

We opened the door and turned the lights on. The barking stopped, but we found both Rottweilers pacing their condo, frothing at the mouth.

"What's the matter, guys?" I said, opening the condo door to pet both dogs.

Josie paused to give them a quick hello, then headed off to check on the rest of the dogs. Moments later she returned with a confused frown on her face.

"What's the matter?" I said.

"Dapper." she whispered.

"Oh, no. Is he okay?" I said, climbing to my feet.

"He's gone."

Chapter 10

It was early, just after sunrise, and Jackson had gotten here as quickly as he could after we finally got in touch with him. He'd had his phone turned off last night when we first discovered that Dapper was missing, and since we had a pretty good idea where Jackson was, Josie and I debated about heading back to my mother's house. But since Dapper's disappearance was the only thing amiss around the Inn, and there wasn't much anyone could do in the middle of the night in minus ten degrees, we eventually decided the initial investigation could wait until morning.

We sipped coffee and watched from the comfort of the Inn while Jackson walked the outside perimeter of the property and then inspected our security system. He spent a lot of time near the fence that bordered the two-acre play area the dogs had at their disposal. Not that any of the dogs were particularly interested in exploring much of the play area in this weather. For the past several weeks, all signs of the dogs' trips outside were confined to a colorful semi-circle that barely reached thirty feet outside the condos. Jackson came back inside stamping snow off his boots. He gratefully accepted the steaming mug of coffee I handed him.

"You look tired, Jackson," Josie said, cocking her head at him and smiling.

"Don't start," I whispered.

"No, actually I slept great," Jackson said. "Once I got past those Sleeping Beauty sheets. I'm surprised I didn't have nightmares."

Josie punched my arm as she stared at Jackson. I was having a hard time believing what I'd just heard myself.

"You and Chef Claire...in my room?" I said.

"What?" Jackson said, then the lightbulb went off. "No, of course not. We were just talking and then we both fell asleep."

"So you're saying that the two of you didn't...?" Josie said.

"Absolutely not. What is wrong with you two?" Jackson said, shaking his head in disgust.

"Well, actually there are a lot of theories floating around," I said.

Josie laughed.

"At least give me a little credit," Jackson said. "And if Chef Claire and I ever decide to take the next step, we certainly won't be doing it in the bedroom of an eight-year-old with a hundred people downstairs."

"Sorry, Jackson," I said.

"Yeah, we're sorry," Josie said. "Better luck next time."

"Josie," he said.

"Yes, Jackson?"

"Shut up," he said, composing himself. "Okay, here's what I can tell at first glance. Your security system was disabled. Whoever it was cut the wiring of the main box outside. I'd like to say they knew what they were doing, but your system is outdated and pretty easy to figure out."

"What does that mean?" I said.

"Basically that they weren't necessarily pros when it comes to this sort of thing, but they probably weren't first-timers either."

"Why were you spending so much time at the back fence?" Josie said.

75

"I found some snowmobile tracks that look fresh," Jackson said. "The recent wind direction has been blowing all the snow up against the fence and now there's about a six-foot high snowbank. And with the woods right behind the fence, a snowmobile would be almost impossible to see from pretty much any direction."

"You know who's an expert on snowmobiles, don't you?" I said.

"Yeah, Rooster," Jackson said. "I just called him, and he said he'd get out here as soon as he could to take a look at the tracks."

I nodded. Jackson was definitely on his game this morning. I guess he did get a good night's sleep.

"How about footprints?" Josie said.

"Yeah, there are two sets leading from the fence to your back door. They're pretty crunchy given how cold it's been, but I think we'll be able to get a couple of good prints."

"So, two guys come in on a snowmobile, disable our security system, break in, and steal Dapper," I said.

"That's my best guess so far," Jackson said. "Sorry, I don't have more for you."

"Poor Dapper," Josie said. "I can't imagine how cold the little guy was on the back of a snowmobile. Last night was brutal."

"I'm betting Dapper was just fine," I said.

"Care to explain that?" Josie said.

"We've both thought there was something special about him since we found him. And if people went to the trouble to steal him in the middle of the night, I'm pretty sure they feel the same way. I imagine they did everything they could to make sure he was safe and sound. And warm."

"Yeah, I can buy that," Josie said, nodding. "And it's certainly better than thinking about the alternative."

"But why would anybody steal that dog?" Jackson said.

"Why would there be people walking around with that tattoo on their hand?" I said.

"Suzy, I hate to remind you, but the guy we found under the ice isn't doing a lot of walking these days," Jackson said.

I told Jackson about my interaction with William Wild at the party. He listened carefully, then another lightbulb went off.

"Is that the guy that all the women were falling over each other to meet last night?" he said.

"Well, I wouldn't say falling over," I said.

"Thankfully the couch broke your fall," Josie said, laughing.

"Wait a minute," I said. "You and Chef Claire were already upstairs by the time we met him."

"I met him earlier before you guys arrived. He was in the kitchen with three other guys he apparently works with, and every female eye was on him," Jackson said. "He seemed like a decent guy. But I didn't notice the tattoo. I must be slipping."

We heard the throaty rumble of a truck pulling into the parking lot in front of the Inn. I headed for the front door and saw Rooster lumbering up the steps. I let him in, and he accepted my hug. He was wearing the same tattered jeans and boots with no socks he'd had on the other day. But he'd swapped out the sweatshirt for a flannel hoodie that had seen better days.

"Thanks for coming over, Rooster," I said. "We're out back. C'mon, I'll get you a cup of coffee."

"That sounds great," Rooster said. "A little splash of Remy would be great if you've got it."

"I think we have some up at the house," I said. "I'll run up."

77

"No, don't worry about it," he said, reaching into his pocket and removing a flask. "Always be prepared."

"Boy Scouts, right?" I said, leading the way to the condo area.

"Marines," he said, offering me the flask.

I smiled and shook my head. He shrugged and took a sip, then put the flask back in his pocket. We entered the condo area, and Rooster greeted Jackson and Josie.

"Hey, Rooster," Josie said. "How's your little guy, Titan, doing?"

"He's perfect," he said, nodding. "Growing like a weed."

I handed him a mug of coffee and Rooster poured from his flask. He took a sip, poured more brandy, then sipped again. Satisfied, he again slipped the flask back in his pocket.

"Okay, you said something about some snowmobile tracks," he said, looking at Jackson.

"Yeah, they're outside," Jackson said.

"No kidding," Rooster said, giving Jackson a small smile that bordered on evil.

"I meant, follow me," Jackson said, glaring at Rooster as he headed for the door.

All four of us walked outside and were immediately buffeted by the strong headwind. Josie and I were wearing multiple layers of clothing topped off by thick parkas. We stared at Rooster who seemed oblivious to the cold as he trudged across the play area sipping his coffee and studying the footprints on the ground.

"You must be cold, Rooster," Josie said.

"Nah," he said as he continued to study the footprints. "I find it refreshing. And the weather is no more than a state of mind."

"I wonder what state that is," Josie whispered.

"My guess is denial," I whispered back.

78

We reached the back fence and Rooster hoisted himself over it and landed waist deep in the snowbank that had collected on the other side. He made his way out of it, then removed his boots, one at a time, and shook the snow out of them before putting them back on. His bare feet were bright pink, but he seemed unfazed.

I shivered just watching him.

"Grizzly Adams, eat your heart out," Josie said, laughing.

Rooster knelt down next to the snowmobile track and removed a tape measure from his pocket. He stretched the tape across the width of the track, frowned, then measured its depth. Then he slid forward on his knees and measured the depth of a different section. He climbed to his feet and glanced around before looking at Jackson.

"Okay, I'm done," Rooster said. "I guess you folks want to do the talking back inside?"

"Yes, please," I said, wheeling around and heading back toward the Inn.

Back inside, I refreshed everyone's coffee, and we settled in my office. Rooster offered his flask to everyone, but we all declined. He sat on the couch next to Jackson and glanced around at the various dog photos on the walls.

"What do you make of it?" Jackson said, removing his parka.

"They probably showed up somewhere between nine and midnight last night," Rooster said, taking a swallow of coffee.

"Can I ask how you know that?" Josie said.

"You can ask me anything you want," Rooster said, smiling at her. "And then I'll pick which questions I want to answer."

Josie laughed, then reached for the candy jar on the desk. She offered the jar to Rooster who shook his head.

"A bit early for candy, isn't it?" he said, topping off his coffee with more brandy.

"I might say the same thing to you," Josie said, laughing as she nodded at his flask.

"It's never too early," Rooster said, taking a sip.

"There you go. Great minds think alike," Josie said, tearing open a bite-sized Snickers.

"The snowmobile track was about half full of snow. And the wind was blowing just hard enough last night to cause the snow to drift a bit. So I'm pretty sure it was around that time," Rooster said.

"Anything else?" Jackson said.

"Given the depth of the track, there were definitely two people on the machine when it showed up," he said.

"When it showed up?" Jackson said.

"Yeah. There are two sets of footprints on the way toward the Inn. But only one on the way back out," Rooster said.

"Really? I completely missed that," Jackson said, frowning.

"Easy thing to do when you're more worried about the cold than finding clues," Rooster said, shrugging.

Jackson glared at him but said nothing.

"And outside I measured the depth of the track in two different spots. The first one was a lot deeper than the second, indicating different weight. That means two people arrived, but only one drove away," Rooster said, staring at Jackson. "Now aren't you glad you called me?"

"Delighted," Jackson deadpanned. "Is there anything else?"

"Yeah, the width of the track is pretty interesting," Rooster said. "It's twenty inches wide. The vast majority of snowmobiles have a fifteen-inch wide track."

"That might be helpful," I said.

"It might," he said, taking a swallow of coffee. "There might be others, but I only know of one machine around here that has a twenty-inch track."

"Do you know who owns it?" I said.

"Yes, I do know. Me," Rooster said. "At least I do now."

Before I could follow up, Jackson decided to move the conversation in a different direction.

"So they showed up when everybody was at the party. I wonder if that was deliberate. You know, part of a plan," Jackson said.

"That would be my guess," Rooster said. "That was a good party."

All three of us stared at him.

"You were at the party?" I said.

"Yeah, but you probably didn't recognize me because I'd cleaned up and put on my good clothes," Rooster said, grinning. "Besides, you were getting pretty busy with the guy on the couch."

"I wasn't getting busy with him," I murmured.

"I thought I warned you about staying away from those people," Rooster said, giving me a hard look.

"What are you talking about?" I said.

"The tattooed ones," Rooster said. "I noticed it when your mom introduced me to him earlier."

"But you never go to parties, Rooster," I said.

"Occasionally, I'll make an exception for people like your mom," he said. "Besides, we had some business to take care of."

I raised an eyebrow at him and waited.

"I had to give her the check for the snowmobile I'd just bought from her," he said, finishing the last of his coffee. "In fact, I need to swing by your mom's place today and pick it up."

"Are you telling me that it was my mother's snowmobile that was here last night?"

"Well, technically, since I gave her the check around seven, it was actually mine by the time they showed up," Rooster said. "But I'm betting that was the machine that was here last night."

"So somebody who was at the party left for a while to come over here and steal Dapper?" Josie said.

"I'll leave all that stuff for you guys to figure out," Rooster said, standing up. "You're much better at those things than I am. Thanks for the coffee. And I'm going to tell you one more time, stay away from those people."

I nodded and waved to him as he headed for the door. Then I called him back.

"Hey, Rooster."

"Yeah?"

"Why did she decide to sell it to you?" I said.

"I think she fell off the other day and scared herself half to death," Rooster said. "I tried to tell her before she bought it that it was too much machine for her to handle."

"She asked you before she bought the snowmobile?"

"Suzy, anybody with half a brain always talks to me first," Rooster said. "It's just too bad more of them don't listen. If you get my point."

I nodded and waved again.

"Okay, I'll see you folks around. And you two, try not to forget what I told you."

Chapter 11

While Rooster hadn't scared us as much as the first time we'd had the conversation about the mysterious tattoo and the people who wore them, he'd still definitely gotten our attention. Given that we'd now been warned to stay away two times by Rooster, someone well versed in criminal behavior and extremely comfortable working on the dark side, it would be logical to assume that we would heed his advice without question. But someone had invaded our private space and messed with one of our dogs; an unforgivable, despicable act that had to be met with direct action.

As far as Josie and I were concerned, the situation had turned personal.

This was the topic on the table, along with a sausage ziti that was a total knee-buckler and a side salad of roasted red peppers and onion, homemade mozzarella, and capicola. The salad was marinating in a garlic-ginger vinaigrette that was addicting, and when I began pondering if I could use it as cologne, I forced myself to put my fork down and take a breath.

I glanced across the table at Josie who apparently was already testing out my vinaigrette as perfume theory. She had it on her face and hands, her blouse, and, if I could have seen under the table, I was pretty sure I'd find more down there. Josie grabbed a hunk of the still warm homemade bread, slid a roasted pepper on top, and then dragged it through the vinaigrette before popping it into her mouth. She caught Chef Claire and I watching her and glanced back and forth at us.

"What?" Josie said, swallowing.

"You're turning the kitchen into a splash zone," I said.

"You're one to talk," Josie said, refocusing on her plate of ziti. "Chef Claire, once again, you amaze me."

"Thanks," Chef Claire said. "I was a bit worried that the ginger might overpower the vinaigrette, but I think it works."

"Yeah, I'd say it works just fine," Josie said, stabbing another of the roasted red peppers.

"I'm getting a bit worried about Freddie," Chef Claire said. "He should have been here by now."

"You told him what you were making for dinner?"

"Yeah."

"Then don't worry, he'll be here," I said, laughing. "I'm sure he's just late because of the weather."

Right after Jackson and Rooster had left this morning, the temperature rose to a balmy ten degrees, then it had started snowing. And it hadn't stopped. Now, a blanket of over two feet of fresh snow greeted us every time we looked out the window, or worse, when we opened the door to let the dogs out. A few hours earlier, Chloe had stood in the doorway, cocked her head, and looked at me like I'd lost my mind. But when Captain, Josie's Newfie, had trotted right out the door to roll around in the snow, Chloe followed, and I closed the door behind them. When I let them back in ten minutes later, they were both covered in a blanket of white that soon turned into a major puddle in the kitchen after they shook themselves off.

Every bit of winter wonder I had experienced and enjoyed through the holiday season had now faded and been replaced by a longing for warm sun and green grass. Long ago, I'd decided that whoever had put our annual calendar together had a good reason for giving February only twenty-eight days. And that reason was winter. I was ready for spring but knew I still had several weeks to wade through before I saw my first flower. And two more feet of snow didn't do much for my mood. Chef Claire, on the other hand, was delighted.

"How about we go cross-country skiing tomorrow?" she said.

Josie and I glanced up from our plates and looked at each other.

"Are you out of your mind?" Josie said, shaking her head. "Try again."

"Oh, come on," Chef Claire said. "It'll be beautiful out there. Just think about all that fresh snow."

"I'm thinking about spending the day in front of the fire reading and sipping hot chocolate between naps."

"What she said," Josie said, nodding as she reached for another piece of bread.

"You guys are no fun," Chef Claire said.

"There's a reason why bears hibernate all winter," Josie said. "By the way, I meant to ask you. How was your sleepover last night?"

"It was pretty sleepy," Chef Claire said. "On the sleep scale, I'd have to give it a ten."

"And on the romance scale?" I said.

"Probably a minus two," Chef Claire said. "I guess that was to be expected because being in your room was a bit creepy. No offense, Suzy, but the Disney sheets don't do much to set the mood."

"It wasn't the Happiest Place on Earth?" Josie said, laughing.

"Based on what I heard about what was happening downstairs on the couch, I don't think it was even the happiest place in the house," Chef Claire said.

"Nothing was happening on the couch," I said, then paused for effect. "There were too many people around."

We laughed until when we heard the unmistakable sound of a snowmobile coming up our driveway. Moments later, we heard a quick knock, and the door opened. Freddie entered, waved, and then removed his snowmobile suit.

"Sorry I'm late," he said, giving Chef Claire a quick kiss on the cheek before sitting down next to her. "I couldn't get my car out of the driveway. It's brutal out there."

"Well, I hope it stops soon," Josie said, winking at me. "We were just talking about going cross-country skiing tomorrow."

"Have fun with that," Freddie said, laughing as he helped himself to the ziti.

"Actually, it was Chef Claire's idea," I said to him before turning to Chef Claire. "You know, if you want some company, Jackson loves to go cross-country."

"What? Oh, yeah," Freddie said. "I think I can make tomorrow work. Sure. That sounds great."

"Smooth," Josie said.

"Did you remember to bring the photos?" I said.

"Yes, I did," Freddie said.

He pulled an envelope from his pocket and slid it across the table. I glanced through the photos quickly.

"He looks a lot better thawed out," I said, sliding one of the photos across the table to Josie.

"He looks familiar," Josie said.

"Really? Let me see that again," I said, taking another look at the photo. "You're right. He does."

Chef Claire glanced over my shoulder at the photo, then shook her head.

"Nope, I got nothing," she said.

"The autopsy results came in this afternoon," Freddie said, through a mouthful of ziti.

"Anything interesting?" I said, giving him my undivided attention.

"Lots," he said, nodding. "He had lungs full of water and a bellyful of Acepromazine."

"What?" Josie said. "Acepromazine?"

"Yeah," Freddie said, reaching for the salad. "You guys aren't missing a couple of bottles by any chance are you?"

"What's Acepromazine?" Chef Claire said.

"It's a dog sedative," Josie said.

"Is it dangerous to humans?" Chef Claire said.

"It certainly is in that size of a dose," Freddie said. "He had enough in him to bring down an elephant."

"I used to live in L.A., and I've seen a lot of weird stuff. So I guess it doesn't surprise me that there are people who would take a dog sedative to try and get high," Chef Claire said.

"There are people out there who smoke catnip and lick cane toads to get high, so anything is possible," Freddie said. "But I don't think that's the case here."

"Why not?" I said, pushing my plate away.

"There were faint but still discernible marks around the guy's neck," he said. "The kind of marks you'd expect to see on a strangulation victim."

"Or on somebody who was having his mouth held open?" Josie said.

"Exactly," Freddie said. "This is fantastic, Chef Claire."

"Thanks. So you think that somebody forced his mouth open and then poured a bottle of dog sedative down his throat?"

87

"That's my working theory at the moment," Freddie said. "But I don't think it's going to matter much what anybody's theory is when it comes to this guy. Nobody, and I mean nobody, has a clue who he was."

"Maybe," I said.

"What's that supposed to mean, Suzy?" Freddie said.

"Nothing," I said, picking up the stack of photos. "Did you check out the logo on the guy's tee shirt?"

"No, I most certainly didn't," Freddie said, laughing. "My job is to figure out why people died and that usually doesn't include me spending a lot of time examining their *clothes*. In fact, my process usually begins after I *remove* their clothes."

"No need to get snarky, Freddie," I said. "It just seems like you're missing an opportunity to identify some possible clues."

"No offense, Suzy," he said. "And I hate tooting my own horn, but in case you haven't noticed, I'm very good at my job."

"And yet you're still unable to transfer your clothing removal skills to the land of the living," Josie deadpanned.

Despite our best efforts, Chef Claire and I burst out laughing. Freddie gave Josie the death stare.

"That was a cheap shot," Freddie said. "Even by your standards."

"Perhaps," Josie said, grinning. "But still funny."

"I braved a blizzard for this," Freddie said, shaking his head. "Pass the wine, please."

"If you're not going to use these," I said, holding up the stack of photos. "I'd like to keep them for a while if you don't mind."

"Knock yourself out. I have another set," he said, taking a sip of wine. "This is good."

"I'm looking for a good house red we can serve at the restaurant," Chef Claire said. "And we're down to a shortlist of three."

"I'm happy to help out with the research," Freddie said.

"Great," Chef Claire said, flashing him a coy smile. "I'll bring a wine bag of another one along with us tomorrow."

"Oh, yeah. Tomorrow," Freddie said. "I can't wait."

Chapter 12

"You can call it anything you want, Chef Claire," Josie snapped. "But as far as I'm concerned, it's blackmail."

"You guys promised," Chef Claire said as she filled a small backpack with sandwiches and other assorted goodies I hadn't gotten a good look at. "You'd think I was asking for a kidney."

"You might as well," Josie said. "Threatening not to cook for a week if we don't go? Now that's downright cruel."

"Chef Claire," I said, "Try to understand that when we agreed to go cross-country skiing with you the next time you went, we never thought there'd be a second time."

I was doing my best to reason with her while still trying to get a good look at what was going into the backpack. If we did end up spending all day trekking through the woods, at a minimum, I wanted to be sure we had adequate nourishment.

"Yeah," Josie said. "Who does something like that twice in the same winter?"

"Well, I love it," Chef Claire. "I hear that the Hidden Woods Trail is beautiful, and we can all use the exercise."

Josie snorted. I stayed silent because Chef Claire was right. I could use a good cardio workout, and trying to work my way through acres of snow while wearing the narrow cross-country skis that had been collecting dust in the garage for three years would certainly do the trick.

"C'mon, it'll be fun," Chef Claire said. "I'm packing a couple of surprises for lunch, and we'll have a picnic."

Josie groaned.

"That's not playing fair, and you know it," Josie said. "You're such a tease."

"Why aren't you going with Freddie?" I said.

"He's working," Chef Claire said.

"What about Jackson?" Josie said.

"No, I can't do that," Chef Claire said, frowning. "I promised Freddie that cross-country would be our thing."

"So we have to suffer just because you made a stupid pact?" I said.

"Yes, you do," Chef Claire said, laughing. "Now, if you're out of lame excuses and able to stop whining, go get ready."

Chef Claire went to the fridge and began removing additional items that all ended up in the backpack. We watched for a few minutes, then glanced at each other and nodded. Beaten, we walked down to the Inn to do a quick check-in with Sammy and Jill before we headed out.

We found them in the condo area rummaging through the supply closet checking inventory levels.

"Good morning, guys," Josie said. "We just thought we'd stop by before we left."

"You lost the argument, huh?" Jill said.

"Yeah, Chef Claire hung tough," I said. "I guess it won't be too bad."

"Compared to what?" Josie said.

"Are you going to be like this all day?" I said.

"Without a doubt," Josie said.

Sammy laughed as he closed the supply closet.

"Let's go check the medicine cabinet," he said to Jill. "I think we're getting low on a couple of things."

I paused when a lightbulb went off in my head.

"Hey, Sammy," I said. "You've been handling medication reorders for a while now, right?"

"Yes," he said, nodding. "Since late summer."

"Do you remember anything odd ever happening?" I said.

"Like what?" Freddie said, sitting down on a stack of fifty-pound bags of dog food.

"I'm not sure," I said. "Maybe a time when you had to reorder something you thought we had a lot of in inventory."

"Yeah, that happens sometimes," Sammy said, smiling at me. "Especially when somebody takes something off the shelves without entering it in the system."

"Why are you looking at me?" I said.

"Because you're the only one who does it," Josie said, laughing.

I looked at Josie, was about to protest, then I caught the smiles on Sammy and Jill's faces.

"Yeah, well," I said. "It gets pretty busy around here at times, and I forget."

"Usually, it happens with things we go through a lot of. You know, bandages, wipes, stuff like that."

"Does it ever happen with medications?" Josie said.

"Only once," Sammy said.

"When was that?" I said.

"It was sometime in the fall I think," Sammy said. "We were down two bottles of the hundred-tablet Acepromazine. I still can't figure out how I missed that."

Josie and I stared at each other.

"Is it possible?" Josie said.

"I guess anything's possible," I said, rubbing my forehead.

"What are you guys talking about?" Jill said, sitting down next to Sammy.

"I'm not sure," I said.

"It was November," Sammy said, looking up from his IPad. "I discovered we were two bottles short and did a reorder."

"That's right," Jill said. "I remember that day."

"Not an easy one to forget," Sammy said, flashing a quick smile at Jill.

Jill's face turned red with embarrassment. Whatever memory had caused it would have to wait. I was focused solely on the missing dog sedative.

"Were we here?" Josie said.

"No, you guys were off that day," Jill said. "I remember because I went looking for you when those two guys came in. Remember those two, Sammy?"

"Who could forget them?" he said, shaking his head.

"What two guys are you talking about?" Josie said.

"Two big mountain-man types came in who said they wanted to adopt a dog. So we gave them a quick tour of the condos. They took a look at all the dogs and said they'd come back later. But they never did," Jill said.

"Did one of them happen to wander off at some point?" I said.

Sammy and Jill looked at each other, then shrugged.

"Maybe," Sammy said.

"Yeah, I guess it's possible," Jill said. "We were talking with one of the guys about Dapper for quite a while in front of his condo. I suppose his buddy might have wandered off at some point."

"It's possible," Sammy said. "But I wouldn't have given it a second thought. We have people in here all the time looking at our

93

dogs. You know, they were looking to adopt a dog, and we had a lot of dogs to choose from. Do you think they could have been the ones who stole the Acepromazine?"

"Anything's possible," I said.

"Why on earth would anybody steal something like that?" Jill said.

I glanced at Josie, and she shook her head just enough for me to notice.

"Who knows?" Josie said. "Some people will steal anything. What happened with these two guys?"

"Well, after we told them that Dapper wasn't eligible for adoption they left, and that was the last we saw of them," Jill said.

"And you noticed the missing bottles sometime after that?" I said to Sammy.

"Yeah, it would have been later," he said. "Those two came in early when we were still doing the morning feeding. And I did the reorder around lunchtime. I'm sorry, but I never thought the two things might be connected."

"Don't worry about it," Josie said. "Nobody would."

"Do you remember anything specific about these guys?" I said.

"Well, they were both really big," Jill said.

"And ugly," Sammy said.

"Yeah, they were really ugly," Jill said. "And hairy."

"They had hair everywhere," Sammy said, nodding. "And one of them had incredibly thick glasses."

"That's right," Jill said. "I remember you saying his lenses must have come from the bottom of a Coke bottle. That was funny."

"Thanks," Sammy said, beaming at Jill.

Jill leaned closer and rested her head on Sammy's shoulder.

"Should I get the hose?" Josie whispered.

"Leave them alone," I whispered back, smiling at the nuzzling couple. "They're in love."

"Yeah, I guess you're right," Josie whispered, then she snapped her fingers. "Hey, guys."

"What?" Sammy said, glancing up.

"You guys look like you could use a break to have some fun," Josie said. "Why don't you take the rest of the day off?"

"And do what?" Jill said.

"Oh, I don't know," Josie said. "Maybe get outside and enjoy the day. Get a little exercise."

"Nice try, Josie," Sammy said, laughing.

"Thanks, but no thanks," Jill said. "We're very happy spending the day here with the dogs."

Josie shook her head and zipped up her jacket.

"I gotta applaud your effort," I said, laughing.

"It was worth a shot," Josie said. "C'mon, let's get this over with."

Chapter 13

I pulled off the two-lane county highway, put my SUV in four wheel drive, then slowly drove up the plowed path that led into the thick woods directly in front of us. The three of us hopped out, removed our skis from the rack on top of the vehicle and put them on. Chef Claire slid the backpack that was holding our lunch over her shoulder and handed both of us a leather wine bag, keeping the third for herself.

"Thanks," I said, adjusting the wine bag until it sat comfortably next to my binoculars that were also hung around my neck. "I think I'm going to need this before we're done."

"It seems strange that this path has been plowed," Chef Claire said.

"It's a designated fire road," I said. "And either the county or the state tries to keep it clear in case there's a fire in the area. The whole area is protected."

"It's beautiful," Chef Claire said, glancing around at the thick forest of pines draped with a blanket of snow. "Freddie would love this."

"It's still not too late to call him," Josie said.

"Will you please stop?" I snapped. "Just suck it up and try to enjoy yourself."

"Okay," she said, gesturing with her hand. "Lead the way, Magellan."

"Uh, that's probably not a good idea," I said, stumbling over my skis. "I'm not very good on these things."

We heard the roar of the snowmobile long before we saw it. It raced out of the woods and across a field in our direction. Then it slowed and eventually stopped right in front of us. Rooster turned the machine off, removed his goggles, and smiled at us. His concession to the weather was a coat and woolen cap. But he was still barefoot underneath his boots sans shoelaces.

"Hello, ladies," he said, giving us a quick wave. "Beautiful day for a ride, huh?"

"Hey, Rooster," I said. "You were flying."

"Yeah, this thing sure is fast," he said. "I almost hit ninety coming across the field."

I shuddered at the thought of my mother driving the powerful machine.

"I'd remind you to be careful not to get lost in the forest," Rooster said. "But as long as you follow your tracks on the way back out, you'll be fine."

"Get lost?" Josie said.

"Yeah, the forest gets pretty thick once you get in there, and it's easy to get yourself turned around," he said.

"This day just keeps getting better," Josie said, pouring a stream of wine from her leather cask into her mouth, then offered it to Rooster. "Feel like a cocktail?"

"Way ahead of you," he said, drinking from a metal flask. "But thanks for the offer. I need to get going. Have fun, but be careful."

Rooster started the snowmobile, waved, then roared off. He was soon a speck in the distance. With Josie leading the way, we began our trek into the forest, slowly working our way across the fresh snow until we were surrounded by large pines.

"This is great," Chef Claire said, glancing over her shoulder. "How are you doing back there?"

"I'm fine," I said, lying through my teeth.

My thighs were cramping, my calves were on fire, and I was sweating like a Sumo wrestler in a sauna.

It started snowing hard as we continued through the forest. An hour later, and barely able to see three feet in front of me through the falling snow, I begged for a break when we came across a snow-covered picnic table with built in seats I recognized from my youth.

"I guess it's a good time to have lunch," Chef Claire said.

We used our hands and ski poles to clear the snow off the table then I collapsed onto the seat and wiped the sweat off my face.

"I'm going to be sore tomorrow," I said, kneading my thighs.

"I hate to tell you, Suzy," Josie said, laughing. "But you won't be able to *walk* tomorrow."

Chef Claire opened the backpack, removed a large thermos, and poured three cups of hot tomato-basil soup. I felt better almost immediately, and my spirits soared when she passed around thick sandwiches filled with assorted cold cuts, sliced Gruyere, and a homemade onion jam.

"Delicious," I said, looking around at the forest that seemed shrouded by the intense snowstorm.

"I had no idea this place existed," Josie said. "It's incredible."

"Solitude," Chef Claire said, pouring a stream of wine from her bag into her mouth.

"Good word," Josie said.

"Yeah," I said. "This is a popular party spot for kids in the summer."

"Well, if I wanted to hide from my parents," Josie said. "This would be a good spot. What else is out here?"

"There's an old quarry you can swim in, and I think I remember a couple of hunting camps around somewhere. Other than that, just a lot of trees and deer."

We finished our lunch in silence as the snow continued to fall. A half hour later, we were again forced to sweep away a couple of inches of snow that had accumulated on top of the table. We then sipped hot coffee and munched on walnut brownies as we made idle chitchat.

"We should probably head back to the car," I said. "It's really coming down."

"Yeah, it looks like we've already got close to another foot," Josie said. "How is that possible?"

We tidied up and put our skis back on. I groaned when I stood up and felt my lower back cramp.

"I'm getting too old for this," I said.

I waited for Josie to comment, but she said nothing. She watched me stare at her then shrugged.

"What?" Josie said.

"No response? No wisecrack?"

"Remember when you said that if I didn't have anything good to say, it was better to just keep quiet?" she said, glancing around.

"Yeah," I said.

"There you go," Josie said. "I've been listening. Okay, Chef Claire. Why don't you take the lead on the way back?"

"Sure," Chef Claire said. "Which way do we go?"

"Just follow the tracks we made on our way in," I said.

Chef Claire glanced around the picnic table, then peered through the heavy snowfall.

"Uh, guys," she said. "I have a question."

"What?" I said.

"What tracks are you talking about?" Chef Claire said.

"You're joking, right?" Josie said, frantically glancing around. "I can't believe it."

"They're gone?" Chef Claire said. "How is that possible?"

"Well, we've been sitting here for a couple of hours," I said. "And it looks like all this fresh snow has already covered our tracks. That's my mistake. I should have been paying closer attention."

"What are we going to do?" Chef Claire said.

"We'll just call somebody. Let's start with Rooster since he has a good idea where we are," I said.

I reached into my pocket to retrieve my phone then stopped.

"I left my phone in the car," I said.

"Me too," Chef Claire said.

Josie removed her phone from her pocket and held it up for us to see.

"Well done," I said.

"Once again, I ride in to save the day," Josie said, removing her gloves.

She pushed a few buttons, frowned, then looked at us sheepishly.

"Guess what I forgot to do last night?" Josie said.

"Recharge your phone?" I whispered.

"You got it in one," Josie said, sliding the phone back into her jacket. "Now what?"

"Well, I'm sure we can figure this out," I said, glancing around, then pointing. "I think we need to head that way."

"I was going to say the exact opposite," Josie said, pointing in the other direction.

100

"I think Suzy's right," Chef Claire said. "I remember when we got here the picnic table was ahead of us and to the right."

"But we moved to the other end of the table to help block the wind, remember?" Josie said.

"Yeah, but we didn't change the direction we were facing when we did that," Chef Claire said. "Did we?"

"I don't think so," I said. "But to be honest, I was so glad just to be sitting down, I wasn't paying much attention."

"This is not good," Josie said.

"Should we pick a direction and stick with it?" Chef Claire said.

"Or maybe we should just stay here," Josie said.

"We'll freeze to death if we stay here," I said.

"Not if we build a shelter and get a fire going," Josie said.

"I've got a lighter," Chef Claire said. "And we could get under the picnic table and pack pine branches and snow around it."

"That could work," Josie said.

"Hang on," I said, racking my memory. "Where are those hunting camps?"

"What are you mumbling about?" Josie said.

"Shhh," I said, sitting back down at the table with my skis splayed at an awkward angle. "I think there are a couple of hunting camps about a mile away from here."

"How do you know that?" Josie said.

"It's a long story," I said.

"All the good ones are," she said.

"I was in high school, and we were having a party out here. And I remember sitting around this picnic table, and then I headed off with my date to get some privacy. We stumbled onto a hunting camp within ten or fifteen minutes after we started walking."

101

"Oooh," Josie said, laughing. "Details, please."

"Shhh," I said, concentrating. "I was sitting at the table in front of the fire. And the fire was near that small group of pines over there, and some people were getting nervous that it was going to spread and set the pine trees on fire. They all started arguing, and we got tired of listening to them and walked off in the opposite direction."

I stood and pointed off into the distance.

"We need to head that way."

"Are you sure?" Josie said.

"I'd go sixty, maybe seventy percent," I said, shrugging.

"That's better than me," Josie said. "I got nothing."

"If we don't find the camp in half an hour, we'll turn around and head back," I said. "If we get moving now, we've got enough daylight to check out both directions. And if all else fails, we can always build the shelter around the picnic table."

"Okay, let's do it," Josie said.

We looked at each other, then nodded. Josie and Chef Claire followed my lurching movements as I made my way through the thick snow and almost zero visibility.

"Chef Claire?" Josie said.

"Yeah."

"You still loving winter?" Josie said.

"Oh, absolutely," she said. "More than ever."

"You really should seek professional help," Josie said.

I laughed as I glanced over my shoulder, then refocused on the wall of swirling white that surrounded me and stretched as far as the eye could see.

Which at the moment was about a foot and a half.

Chapter 14

Although a bit spotty, overall, my memory had served me well. While I wasn't sure about the exact year I'd been out here with a boy whose name I couldn't recall, I had remembered the approximate location of the hunting camp. Maybe when you're staring straight down the barrel at hypothermia, followed by frostbite and the prospect of your frozen body not being found until spring, your brain somehow manages to bring back the truly important information you need for survival.

Our visibility remained almost non-existent, and we'd been forced to remove and carry our skis, which had become useless when we hit waist-high snowdrifts that would have looked great on a postcard but made skiing impossible. It started snowing even harder, something I wouldn't have believed possible an hour ago. Now standing chest-high in snow, I was finally able to pick out the outline of the camp through my binoculars.

"There it is. About a hundred feet ahead just off to the right," I said, handing the binoculars to Josie. "Put the strap over your head."

"Why?" Josie said, peering through the glasses.

"Because if you drop them in this snow, there's a good chance we won't ever find them."

"Okay, good point," Josie said, draping the strap over her head. "I can barely make it out, but it looks like the shape of a house. What do you think we should do?"

"Gee, I don't know, Josie," I snapped. "Maybe head over there and go inside?"

"There's no need to get snarky," she said.

"I'm standing up to my chest in a snowdrift, freezing my butt off, and wearing a snow-packed bra. If I can't be a little snarky now, when can I?"

"Another good point," Josie said, handing the binoculars back.

"This is incredible," Chef Claire said, trudging forward until she was standing on my other side. "What an adventure."

"Chef Claire," I whispered. "While I appreciate your newfound love for all things winter, I need you to do something for me."

"Sure. What is it?"

"Shut up."

Josie snorted. I glanced at Chef Claire who was laughing even as the relentless storm continued to blanket her in white. I looked through the binoculars then stopped when I heard the familiar mouse-crinkle of foil being unwrapped. I lowered the binoculars and stared at Josie.

"Really?"

"What? You know I never go anywhere without them," Josie said, holding one of the objects out for me. "You want one? They're frozen."

"Oh, I love frozen Snickers," I said, accepting her offer. "Maybe just one."

"Chef Claire, do you want a bite-sized?" Josie said.

"No, I'm good. Thanks," Chef Claire said. "So we're just going to break in?"

"Yeah, but it's okay," I said. "It's what anybody would expect us to do given the circumstances."

Again, I looked through the binoculars to determine the path of least resistance that would take us to the front door, then stopped.

"That's odd," I said.

"What?" Josie said.

"There's smoke coming out of the chimney," I said.

"Maybe it's a couple of hunters," Chef Claire said.

"If it is, they're hunting out of season," I said.

"It wouldn't be the first time we've seen that," Josie said.

"No, it wouldn't," I said. "But it does seem strange for somebody to be out here in the middle of February."

"Allow me just a moment to point out the incredible irony of your last statement," Josie deadpanned.

"Yeah, good point," I said, laughing. "Okay, let's head for the front door. We'll just knock and see who answers."

"Isn't that what somebody always says in a horror movie right before they get their head lopped off?" Josie said.

"Really?" I said, glancing through the binoculars. "A horror movie? You're going to go there? Wait, the front door is opening."

"What do you see?" Josie said.

"You're not going to believe it," I said, handing the binoculars to her.

"Dapper?" Josie whispered. "Wow. Talk about your dumb, blind luck." She laughed while continuing to stare through the glasses. "He won't get off the porch."

"Can't blame him for that," I said. "I certainly wouldn't want to pee outside today."

"Suzy, I hate to tell you," Josie said, handing me back the binoculars. "But if we don't get out of this snow pretty soon, you aren't going to have a choice."

"Yet another good point. You're on your game today," I said. "What did Sammy and Jill say about the two guys who'd come to the Inn? Something about the glasses one of them was wearing?"

"Yeah, the glasses were so thick they called them Coke bottle lenses," she said.

"Well, there he is," I said. "And he doesn't look very happy with Dapper at the moment."

"This is our chance," Josie said.

"To do what?" Chef Claire said.

"To get Dapper back, of course," Josie said.

"How do you plan on doing that?" Chef Claire said.

"Watch," Josie said. "Suzy, keep the binoculars on Coke Bottle. We need to see what he does."

"You got it," I said, focusing on the agitated man wearing slippers and a pair of flannel pajamas.

Josie whistled sharply once. I focused the binoculars on Dapper who now had his head cocked.

"Did he hear me?" Josie said.

"Yeah. He's on point," I said.

Josie whistled again, and Dapper trotted down the steps and looked around.

"Okay, it's now or never," I said.

She whistled a third time, then called the dog.

"Dapper! Come here, boy."

The dog confirmed the location of Josie's voice and began a mad dash through the snow. And if I hadn't been so concerned about Dapper's wellbeing, I would have laughed at the sight of him and his trademark scarf trailing behind him as his head appeared out of the pile of snow, then disappeared from sight only to pop back up moments later.

"Good boy. Over here," Josie said.

"Get back here, you stupid dog," Coke Bottle said.

"I don't think the guy can hear us," Josie said.

"That makes sense," I said, lowering the binoculars. "We're downwind."

Dapper completed his hundred foot journey and jumped right into Josie's outstretched arms. He licked her face, pawed at her arms, then squirmed out of her arms. He paused to squat and pee, then climbed back into her arms.

"What a good boy. We missed you," Josie said, then glanced over at me. "What's Coke Bottle doing?"

"At the moment, he's standing on the porch wondering what the heck just happened and where Dapper went," I said.

"We need to take him out," Josie said.

"Absolutely," I said.

"What are you talking about?" Chef Claire said.

"We need to take him out," Josie repeated.

"How do you suggest we do that?" Chef Claire said.

"I think we should use this weather to our advantage," Josie said.

"Perfect," I said. "And combine it with the element of surprise."

"Yeah. Just give me a minute to think this through," Josie said, handing Dapper to Chef Claire.

"Just don't take too long," I said, trying to adjust the Lycra bodysuit I was wearing underneath my ski suit. "I think I just went up another cup size."

"Let me have the binoculars," Josie said.

I handed them to her, and she took a moment to confirm that Coke Bottle was still standing on the porch before she surveyed the rest of the area.

"There's a storage shed about fifty feet to our left," Josie said. "It looks like it's where they keep their snowmobile and firewood. Let's

107

work our way over there. Then we'll use Dapper to get Coke Bottle to wander over."

"Then what?" I said.

"I'm not sure," Josie said. "But getting his glasses off would be a good start."

"Good idea," I said. "Maybe we could tackle him?"

"It may come to that," Josie said. "But I think we should try to separate him from his glasses first before we get too close. He's a big guy, and I don't like the thought of him getting his hands on me and holding my head under four feet of snow."

"I'll do it," Chef Claire said.

We both looked at her and waited for her to continue.

"If I can get close, I can hit him with a snowball," Chef Claire said.

"That's right," I said. "You used to play softball in college. You think you can take him out with a snowball?"

"Piece of cake," Chef Claire said.

"Mmmm, cake," Josie said. "I wonder if he has anything good to eat inside."

"Focus, please," I said, chuckling softly. "There's only one problem with your plan, Chef Claire. This snow is too fluffy. You can't make a snowball out of this stuff."

"No, but I can certainly make a good one out of that," she said, pointing at the yellow patch that Dapper had recently provided.

Josie and I smiled at each other.

"A yellow ice ball in the face," Josie said. "Chef Claire, that is a brilliant and extremely deviant idea. I'm so proud of you."

"Thanks," Chef Claire said, grabbing a large handful of the yellow snow.

"Okay," I said. "Let's work our way toward that shed, and we'll see if we can get Coke Bottle's attention. There's probably a section that's been packed down by their trekking back and forth to get firewood. If you can find it, Chef Claire, you should be able to get some solid footing."

"Got it," Chef Claire said, packing the yellow ice ball until it was about the size of a softball.

"You sure you'll be able to hit him?" Josie said.

"Hit him? I was all-conference at third base," she said. "With my arm, he'll be lucky if I don't kill him."

"What do you think we should do with him after that?" Josie said.

"Normally, I'd say just leave the dognapper for the wolves to find," I said. "But we don't want to give him any chance for revenge."

"Yeah, good point," Josie said, nodding. "I imagine getting hit in the face with a frozen ball of dog pee might make him a bit cranky."

I glanced through the binoculars and saw that Coke Bottle was still baffled by the dog's disappearance. But he had made his way down off the porch and was doing his best to see through the snowstorm. We slowly worked our way toward the shed and eventually made our way out of the snowdrift onto a section where the snow only came up to our knees. Chef Claire put Dapper down, and he glanced around at all three of us but remained by our side.

"I've got an idea," I said, removing the backpack from Chef Claire's shoulders. "We can use the straps on this to tie his hands behind his back."

"And if that doesn't work," Josie said, selecting a piece of firewood from a large stack. "This will do the trick."

"Okay, let's get this done," I said, again cringing from the snowpack that was stuffed inside my bra but starting to melt.

109

"Dapper," Josie said. "Can you say hello?"

The dog gave Josie one sharp bark. I glanced through the binoculars, and Coke Bottle was now looking in our direction.

"He sure does have a big bark for such a little guy," Chef Claire said as she worked her way onto a relatively stable patch of snow. Josie followed her and stood a few feet behind Chef Claire.

"Don't you need to warm up with a few practice throws?" Josie said.

"No, I think I've got this one," Chef Claire said, laughing as she rubbed the shoulder of her throwing arm.

"Let's go," I said, shivering. "I've got a mountain stream running into my navel."

"Dapper," Josie said. "Can you say hello?"

Again, he barked once loudly. I peered through the binoculars, then lowered them.

"Okay," I said. "He's on his way. Get ready."

We waited for several seconds; then Coke Bottle appeared out of the blinding snowstorm.

"You stupid dog. Where are you?"

Chef Claire took a step forward, cocked her arm and waited.

"Who are you calling stupid?" Josie said.

Coke Bottle was startled and turned toward Josie's voice. Then Chef Claire fired the yellow ice ball from no more than ten feet away. It hit him in the face, shattered his glasses, his nose, and probably a couple more facial bones with very long names.

Coke Bottle went down.

And he went down hard.

"Wow," Josie said. "Great shot."

We surrounded the unconscious man whose blood was turning the ground into a Daliesque portrait of the Canadian flag. The three of us flipped him over onto his back and tied his hands tight with the straps I'd cut off the backpack.

"What do we do with him?" Josie said.

"Let's drag him into the shed," I said. "Once we're sure it's safe, we can come back and get him. We don't want him to freeze to death."

"Or, we could just leave him," Josie said.

"Josie," I said, my voice rising a notch.

"I'm just kidding," she said. "But I hate dognappers."

"Not as much as you'd hate jail," Chef Claire said.

Josie and I weren't going to argue that point with her. Last summer, Chef Claire had been falsely accused of murder and had spent some time in prison until we'd helped get the situation sorted out.

We dragged Coke Bottle into the shed and found a blanket and some rope inside the snowmobile's storage area under the seat. We laid him down on the seat, wrapped the blanket around him, then used the rope to tie him to the snowmobile. I stepped back to admire our handiwork and nodded.

"He's not going anywhere," I said, squirming and wiggling my legs as my bladder threatened to burst and the melting snow inside my bra continued its southern journey.

"Kind of an odd time to start boogying, isn't it?" Josie said, staring at me. "What is that? Your happy dance?"

"Shut up," I said. "We need to get inside."

"What's the plan?" Josie said.

"Given the current state of my bladder, I'd like to suggest swift and direct action," I said, selecting a piece of firewood from the stack.

"We'll position ourselves around the front door and use Dapper to get the other guy's attention."

"Since I'm not exactly sure how that's going to work, how about I just follow your lead?" Josie said.

"Don't worry," I said. "You'll know it as soon as you see it. Now choose your weapon."

Josie and Chef Claire each selected a piece of firewood, and we crossed the path in single file with Dapper leading the way. I commanded Dapper to stay at the bottom of the steps, and we slowly made our way onto the porch, and I positioned myself on one side of the door and motioned for Josie and Chef Claire to stand on the other. I nodded at Josie.

"Dapper," Josie whispered. "Can you say hello?"

Dapper barked loudly once and continued to stare up at us with his head cocked.

Moments later, the front door opened, and a large man's head appeared in the doorway.

"You stupid dog. There you are," the man said. "What took you so long, Walter? Walter?"

The man stepped onto the porch, and I swung the piece of firewood I was holding. It struck him in the back of the head, and he went down like a sack of potatoes. Dapper raced up the steps and bit the man's hand hard.

The man didn't even notice.

"Let him go, Dapper," Josie said, laughing. "What a good dog."

"Nice swing," Chef Claire said. "Did you ever play ball?"

"Nope," I said, pulling a section of rope from my pocket and kneeling down next to the man. "My mother didn't think it was ladylike."

112

"That's too bad," Chef Claire said. "You crushed that one."

"Well, let's hope not," I said, examining the lump on the back of the man's head. "Help me pull his hands back."

We tied his hands and feet then dragged him inside the hunting camp. We found another length of rope in one of the closets and Josie secured him to a large pipe that ran along one wall. When we were confident he wasn't going anywhere, I stood up and removed my ski suit, then unzipped the Lycra body suit. I reached into my bra and used both hands to remove two large snowballs. I held them up for Josie and Chef Claire to see before tossing them into the fireplace.

"You know, Suzy," Josie deadpanned. "I think there are easier ways to move up a cup size."

"You're not funny."

"Disagree."

Josie and Chef Claire laughed as they headed out to drag Coke Bottle back inside. While they were gone, I made a trip to the bathroom then stood by the fire to warm up and get reacquainted with Dapper. I made sure he had water, then grabbed three bottles of water for us from the fridge. A few minutes later, Chef Claire and Josie returned and dragged Coke Bottle across the floor and tied him up next to the other man. They were slowly regaining consciousness but remained groggy.

We sat down in the living room and stretched out on a couple of surprisingly comfortable couches. I glanced around at the high ceiling and the open living area.

"This place is pretty nice," I said.

"Yes, it is," Josie said. "I thought you'd been here before."

"No, we couldn't find the key, so we decided to just go swimming in the quarry."

"I wonder who owns it," Josie said.

"That would probably tell us a lot," I said.

"So what do we do now?" Chef Claire said.

"Find a phone. Make a call. Then hope that somebody can find us before spring arrives," I said.

"I doubt if anybody is going to be able to find us tonight. It's going to get dark soon," Josie said.

"Yeah, you're right," I said. "I guess we're spending the night with those two. What do you say, Josie? I think Coke Bottle is just your type."

"Funny."

"If we're going to be stuck here, then I'm going to take a look around and see what sort of food we've got," Chef Claire said.

I glanced at Josie who nodded back.

"I could eat."

Chapter 15

We found a cell phone on the kitchen counter, and I called Jackson first. He answered on the third ring, and I put the phone on speaker and sat down on the couch.

"This is Jackson."

"Hey, it's me," I said.

"Suzy? Sorry, I didn't recognize the number," he said.

Josie poured from a half-full, half-gallon jug of cheap wine she'd found that tasted surprisingly good and Chef Claire placed a tray of snacks on the coffee table in front of us. I grabbed a piece of cheese and a couple of crackers.

"Where are you?" Jackson said. "I tried calling you earlier, but nobody answered at your house or down at the Inn. I was getting worried, what with this storm and all. I just heard on the news that we're looking at four, maybe five feet."

"Yeah, it's really coming down," I said, glancing out the window at the snowfall that was continuing to accumulate at an alarming rate.

"Just be glad you aren't out in it," he said, laughing.

"Jackson, you have no idea how happy I am about that," I said.

I took a few minutes to explain where we were and how we'd got there, then paused to take a sip of wine while Jackson responded.

"So you guys are safe?" he said, wrapping up his initial reaction.

"Yeah, we're fine, Jackson," Chef Claire said.

"We're certainly doing better than the two dognappers," Josie said, then glanced at the two men who were now conscious and listening to our conversation. "Yeah, that's right, morons. I'm talking about you."

"Tell me exactly where you are," Jackson said.

"You'll see my SUV parked a couple of hundred feet up the path after you make the turn off Route 3 onto the Hidden Woods Trail. Do you remember that picnic area everybody used to hang out around in the summer?"

"Sure," Jackson said, laughing. "I remember striking out many times with the girls at those parties."

"Then I have to say, Jackson, I don't like your chances with Chef Claire," Josie said, grinning at us.

"What are you talking about?" he said.

"I saw her fastball earlier today," Josie said. "You'll never hit it in a million years."

The three of us roared with laughter. Well versed with our tendency to lose focus when we were on the phone, I heard Jackson shuffling papers on the other end of the line as he waited for us to finish.

"Maybe you can explain that one to me later," Jackson said. "So, you're near that picnic area?"

"We were," I said. "You remember where the swimming quarry is?"

"Sure," Jackson said.

"There are a couple of hunting camps near there. Less than a mile from the picnic area," I said.

"Sure. I know where Rooster's camps are," he said.

"What?" I said. "Rooster owns this place?"

"Yeah. Rooster owns most of the land around that area. At least he always has."

"I did not know that," I said, glancing at Josie and Chef Claire.

"How about that?" Jackson said. "You must be slipping."

"Funny."

"Let me call, Rooster," he said. "And we'll see if we can get out there tonight."

"No," I said. "It's way too dangerous for you guys to be out on snowmobiles in this storm in the dark. We'll be okay here for the night."

"Let me think about that," Jackson said. "But if we can't make it out tonight, make sure you guys sleep in shifts and have at least one person keeping an eye on your two guests at all times."

"Will do," I said. "Okay, we'll see you soon."

"Yes, you will," he said. "So please don't do anything stupid."

"You mean, like go cross country skiing in a blizzard?" Josie said, glancing at Chef Claire.

"Exactly," Jackson said. "Be safe."

He ended the call, and I grabbed another piece of cheese.

"I'm going to pay for this one, aren't I?" Chef Claire said.

Josie stared at Chef Claire for a long time with an odd smile on her face. Eventually, Chef Claire looked at me.

"She's doing that *if you don't have anything good to say, don't say anything* routine, isn't she?" Chef Claire said.

"Yup," I said, rubbing my thighs that continued to ache and throb. "But it's nothing that French onion soup and one of your roast dinners won't solve."

I grimaced as I got up off the couch and grabbed a metal folding chair as I approached the two men who were staring up at me. I sat down a few feet away from them and did my best to smile at them.

"So how do you guys know Rooster?" I said.

117

"Who?" Coke Bottle said.

Without his glasses, he wasn't quite able to focus on me. His face was a bloody mess, and he continued to squint in my general direction, and, apparently, wasn't in the mood to chat. I looked at the one I'd hit in the back of the head with the piece of firewood.

"Got a headache?" I said.

"Maybe," he said, glaring at me.

"You got any aspirin around here?" I said.

"Maybe."

"Suit yourself," I said.

"Medicine cabinet in the bathroom," he said, grimacing as he tried to sit more upright.

"I should probably take a look at them," Josie said, kneeling down in front of Coke Bottle.

"Are you a doctor?" he said.

"Actually, I'm a vet," Josie said. "Given your species, I guess it's your lucky day."

"You're going to pay for this, lady," Coke Bottle said, squinting in the direction of Josie's voice.

"Hey, I didn't throw it," Josie said.

"What did I get hit with anyway?"

"Ice ball," Josie said.

"I thought I saw a flash of yellow at the last second," he said.

"You did," Josie said, then noticed the look of confusion on the man's face. "Think about it."

He did, and anger eventually replaced his look of confusion. Josie hopped to her feet and headed into the kitchen area and turned on the tap. She returned a few minutes later holding two towels she'd soaked in hot water. She began cleaning Coke Bottle's face and examining his wounds. He grimaced but hung tough. When she finished, she knelt down and closely inspected his face.

"Well, the good news is that I don't think any of your facial bones are broken. But make sure to ask the cops during questioning if you can get an x-ray. And I'm afraid you're going to be breathing out of your mouth for a while."

"And my glasses?"

"I'm sorry," Josie deadpanned, shaking her head. "But I don't think they made it."

"Lady, you ain't funny," Coke Bottle said.

"Disagree," she said, sliding over to the other man. "Let's have a look at you. You got a name?"

"Jerry," the man grunted.

"Okay, Jerry the Dognapper," Josie said, gently wiping the bump on the man's head with a warm towel. "The bleeding has stopped, but you might need a couple of stitches. And you probably have a concussion. That was quite a shot you took."

"Yeah. And don't worry, I won't forget," he said, glaring at me.

"Let me see that hand," Josie said, leaning forward to take a look at his tied hands. "It's bleeding a bit, but you'll survive."

"What happened to my hand?" Jerry said.

"Dog bite," Josie said.

"I don't remember getting bit by a dog," Jerry said, frowning.

"You were taking a bit of a *nap* when it happened," I said.

Josie snorted and sat back down on the floor.

"So how do you know Rooster?" I said for the second time.

"Lady, I don't have a clue who you're talking about," Jerry the Dognapper said.

I paused when I caught a whiff of something coming from the kitchen. Both men noticed it as well. I glanced over at Josie, but she'd already disappeared. I saw her hovering next to Chef Claire by the stove. Then Chef Claire shooed her away, and Josie returned. She unfolded another of the metal chairs and sat down next to me.

"Beef stew and homemade biscuits," Josie said, shaking her head. "Right out of thin air. How does she do it?"

"Never question true genius," I said, then turned back to Jerry. "If I have to ask you a third time, I'm going to get cranky. Rooster?"

"He's a friend of mine," Jerry said.

"How about that? Me too," I said.

"Really? You're a friend of Rooster?"

"Yeah. We're good friends," I said. "Does that surprise you?"

"Kinda, yeah," he said, wincing. "Why'd you hit me so hard?"

"Why did you steal our dog?" I said.

"That was your dog?" Jerry said, then stopped. "I mean, we didn't steal any dog. We found him."

I decided to push the envelope and go with a big lie.

"Our surveillance cameras tell a different story," I said.

"I told you they probably had cameras," Coke Bottle blurted.

"You idiot, shut up," Jerry said. "She was bluffing."

"Oh," Coke Bottle said, squinting hard as he glanced around. "Yeah, we found that dog."

Jerry the Dognapper shook his head, then looked up at me.

"We do some work for Rooster from time to time," he said.

My stomach dropped, and I looked at Josie who seemed to be having the same reaction.

"Were you working for him this time?" I whispered.

"You mean when we... *found* the dog?"

120

"Yeah."

"No, Rooster would never have anything to do with something like that," Jerry said. "He's a dog lover."

I relaxed and smiled, then sat back in my chair and crossed my legs. My thighs screamed at me, and I was forced to change positions.

"So who are you working for?" Josie said.

"Lady, I have no idea what you're talking about," Jerry said.

"Yeah, like we're going to tell you who we're working for," Coke Bottle said.

"Will you just keep your mouth shut?" Jerry said, glaring at his companion.

"What are you yelling at me for?" Coke Bottle said. "I didn't tell her anything."

Jerry the Dognapper exhaled loudly and looked at me.

"Cousin," he said, nodding at Coke Bottle. "What can you do?"

"Sure, sure," I said, nodding right along with him. "Family."

"Yeah. Look, even if I could tell you who hired us, you don't want to know. These are some nasty creatures."

Considering the source of that comment, it definitely resonated with me. Then I remembered Rooster telling us the same thing.

"Well, you'll have lots of time to talk once you two are in prison," I said.

"Oooh, stop it, lady. You're scaring me," Jerry said, giving me a big smile. "A charge of simple B&E and a stolen dog. We'll be out on bail before my lawyer can stop laughing."

"Probably," I said. "Unless the cops decide to pin a murder charge on you for the guy they found under the ice."

Finally, I had his undivided attention.

"What are you talking about? What guy?" Jerry said.

"Oh, didn't you hear?" I said, watching his face closely. "Look at that, Josie. I think our new friend just saw his life flash before his eyes."

"I didn't kill anybody. And I don't know anything about a guy under the ice," Jerry said. "All we were asked to do was to grab the dog and keep him in a safe place until we heard from them."

"Now that I think about it," Josie said. "Didn't the police say there were looking for two men who fit their description?"

"I think you're right, Josie," I said, climbing to my feet.

"You're bluffing again," Jerry said.

"I guess we'll see when the police get here in the morning," Josie said, then looked at me. "Do you smell biscuits?"

"I do," I said. "Let's go see what Chef Claire is up to."

We started toward the kitchen area, but stopped and turned around when we heard Jerry calling after us.

"Yes, Jerry?" I said, smiling down at him.

"Look, I still think you're bluffing, but maybe we can make a deal," Jerry said.

"Why would we make a deal?" I said. "The only thing we wanted was the dog back. You'll need to save your offer of a deal for the cops."

We resumed our stroll toward the stove.

"Hey! Hey, you!"

I turned around and frowned at him.

"That's way too loud, Jerry. You need to dial it down a notch," I said. "We've had a very long day and would really like to enjoy a little peace and quiet."

"Well, it doesn't look like that's going to happen, does it?" Jerry said. "Now get back over here!"

"Tenacious little moron, isn't he?" Josie said.

"Yeah. I guess it's time to bring in the big guns," I said.

"You're a couple of weirdos. What is wrong with you two?"

"Actually, Jerry, there are several working theories about that question floating around," Josie said.

"What are you talking about?" Jerry said, blinking repeatedly.

Josie removed a small blanket that was draped over the couch, folded it carefully, then placed it on one of the metal chairs in front of the two men.

"Dapper," she said, patting the blanket. "Come here, boy."

Dapper trotted across the room and hopped up onto the blanket. Josie rubbed his head, then he stretched out with his head propped on his front paws and growled at the men.

"Why don't you keep an eye on them while we eat dinner, Dapper?" Josie said. "Can you say hello?"

Dapper barked once, and both men slunk back as far as they could against the wall and grimaced. Josie and I made our way into the kitchen area.

"It smells fantastic," I said, peering into the pot where the stew was gently bubbling.

"They must have done a recent shop," Chef Claire said. "In case they have trouble getting us out of here, we've got enough food for several days."

"Oh, let's hope it doesn't come to that," Josie said, then glanced at me. "Why did you turn their offer of a deal down so quickly?"

"Because they'll talk a lot faster if the real possibility of a murder charge gets tossed in their lap," I said. "Besides, I don't think we need their offer at this point. We've got everything we need right here."

"Suzy, I'm exhausted and very hungry," Josie said. "How about we skip the cryptic route tonight?"

"Fair enough," I said, grabbing the cell phone off the counter. "It's not password protected."

"So?"

"So, with the push of a button, we'll have a list of every call they've recently made," I said, scrolling through the call registry.

"Well done," Josie said. "I should have figured that one out."

"Well, you are exhausted and very hungry," I said, laughing. "It's completely understandable."

"I appreciate that," she said, rifling through one of the kitchen drawers until she found pen and paper. "Okay, you read, I'll write."

Chapter 16

Around 5 AM, I was taking my turn on guard duty and doing my best to stay awake when I heard the throaty roar of an engine off in the distance. I got up from my chair and limped to the kitchen to look out the window at the lit front porch. I decided that between the darkness and the five-foot blanket of snow that had fallen, I was wasting my time. I refilled Dapper's water bowl, started the coffee maker, then sat back down. Dapper, who hadn't moved from the chair since he'd laid down hours earlier, glanced over at me, then refocused on Jerry the Dognapper and Coke Bottle who were still secured to the pipe and softly snoring.

The roar of the engine continued to get louder, and I debated about waking Josie and Chef Claire who were sound asleep on couches on either side of me. Before I could make my decision, Josie stirred then sat up and rubbed her eyes. She looked around the room and caught my eye.

"Morning," she said. "I thought I heard something."

"You did," I said, getting my first whiff of the coffee. "It sounds like a snowmobile."

"The rescue team is here early."

"Yes," I said, rubbing my thighs. "Let's just hope they're coming to rescue *us*."

"Now there's a cheery thought to get the day started," she said as she climbed to her feet. Then she winced. "Oh, I hurt everywhere."

Chef Claire rolled over and opened her eyes.

"I smell coffee," she said.

"Good morning," I said. "It'll be ready soon. Did you get some sleep?"

"Yeah, I was out," Chef Claire said, sitting up and grimacing. "Man, that was a workout yesterday."

"Do all of us a favor and remember this moment the next time you start thinking about asking us to go cross-country skiing," Josie said to Chef Claire.

"Geez, Josie," I said, shaking my head. "It's five in the morning, don't start."

"Thank you," Chef Claire said, heading for the kitchen. "Maybe you'll feel better after coffee."

"Well, I certainly couldn't feel any worse," Josie said.

I glared at Josie, and she shrugged then stretched back out on the couch, moaning all the way down.

"What a baby," I said.

The roar of the engine got close, then it stopped. Chef Claire glanced out the window, then tapped on it and waved.

"It's Rooster," Chef Claire said. "It must be nasty out there, he's wearing snow boots.

"Is anybody else with him?" I said, hobbling toward the door.

"It doesn't look like it," Chef Claire said, turning back to the coffeemaker.

I waited for the knock and then opened the door. A snow-covered Rooster was standing under the porch light brushing the snow off and stamping his feet. He stepped inside, and I quickly closed the door to keep the cold air out then gave him a hug.

"Thanks for coming, Rooster," I said. "Is anybody with you?"

"No, but they're on their way," he said, glancing around the camp. "Sorry, it took me awhile to get out here. I had to get organized and then wait a couple of hours for the snow to let up."

"Quite the storm, huh?" I said.

"It's been a while since I've seen anything like it," Rooster said. "You guys are lucky you found this place. If you hadn't, we might be doing a very different kind of search and rescue mission today."

Chef Claire handed Rooster a mug of steaming coffee. He smiled and nodded at her.

"Thanks for saving us, Rooster," Chef Claire said, patting his arm.

"No problem. People around here would never forgive me if anything happened to you, Chef Claire," he said. "Morning, Josie."

He laughed as he watched Josie hobble her way across the room.

"Hey, Rooster. How bad is it out there?" Josie said, pouring coffee.

"It's bad, but we'll get you home safe and sound," he said, walking into the living room. "Now, let's have a look at the two critters that had the nerve to break into my hunting camp."

When Rooster got his first look at the two men tied to the pipe, he glared at them and shook his head. Rooster nudged both of them with one of his boots and took a sip of coffee.

"I should have known," Rooster said as he waited for them to wake up.

"So you do know these guys," I said.

"Yeah. Sad to say, but yes," Rooster said, giving both men a harder nudge with his boot. "Hey, wake up."

Coke Bottle opened his eyes and squinted as he glanced around the room.

"Rooster? Is that you, Rooster?" Coke Bottle said.

127

"What happened to your face?" Rooster said, staring at the man's cuts and bruises and nose that was swollen to twice its normal size.

"I got hit with a snowball," Coke Bottle whispered.

Rooster chuckled.

"A snowball did that to you?" he said, glancing over his shoulder at us. "That must have been some snowball."

"Well," Josie said. "It was traveling at a rather high rate of speed."

"And made of ice," I said.

"Ice? Good," Rooster said, turning back to the two men. "Morning, Jerry."

"Hey, Rooster," Jerry the Dognapper said, cowering like a chastised puppy. "How you doing?"

"I'm just great, Jerry," Rooster said. "Just great. Of course, if I were to complain, it would be about having to go outside in the worst blizzard in forty years to clean up another one of your messes."

Josie and I sat down on the couch and listened closely.

"*Another* mess?" I whispered.

"Yeah, I heard," Josie whispered back. "Interesting."

"Look, I'm sorry, Rooster," Jerry said. "But you said we could use the camp anytime we wanted."

"To hunt, you moron," Rooster said. "Not to do stupid stuff. Didn't I warn you about not getting involved with those people?"

Another warning from Rooster about *those people*. I made a mental note to do some real digging into who he was referring to as soon as I got home.

"Yeah, you did," Jerry said. "We're sorry, Rooster."

Rooster shook his head and looked like he was about to kick the two men again for a different reason. Then he looked at us on the couch.

"My brother has something he'd like to say to you. Don't you, Jerry?"

"Your brother?" I said, stunned by the news.

"Yeah," Rooster said, shrugging. "But what can you do?"

"Sure, sure," I said, nodding sympathetically. "Family, huh?"

"Yeah," Rooster said, glaring at Jerry. "So what do you have to say to Suzy and Josie?"

"Sorry," Jerry said.

"Sorry for what?" Rooster said.

"For breaking into your place," Jerry said.

"And?" Rooster said.

"And we're sorry we stole your dog."

"Okay. Is that it?" Rooster said.

Jerry frowned, then looked up at Rooster.

"I think that's it," Jerry said.

"Don't forget the two bottles of medicine we took the first time we were there," Coke Bottle said, squinting and glancing around in the general direction of the voices.

"What?" Rooster said.

"Yeah, that's right," Jerry said. "I forgot about that one. Sorry."

"You stole dog medicine?" Rooster said, bewildered by the idea.

"Yeah, it's supposed to make dogs relax," Coke Bottle said. "And I was out of weed. So I figured it might be worth a shot. You know, just up the dose a bit. But it was a crappy buzz."

"I should probably ask what is wrong with you," Rooster said, bewildered. "But I stopped asking that question a long time ago."

129

"You ate both bottles of that stuff?" Josie said.

"Nah," Coke Bottle said. "I ended up throwing most of it away after I tried it."

"How much did you take?" Josie said.

"Just a couple of big handfuls," he said, squinting.

"Geez, you probably shouldn't have done that," Josie said.

"Why not?" Coke Bottle said, scanning the room trying to focus on Josie.

"It's just not a smart thing to do," Josie deadpanned. "But I guess we can't blame you for that, huh?"

Rooster snorted and smiled at Josie.

As far as the sedative itself was concerned, Acepromazine was briefly used on humans in the 1950's as an anti-psychotic drug but was now used strictly with animals. A normal dog dose probably wouldn't create any major problems for a person, but, like everything else in life, too much of anything can be bad for you. And if this despicable moron, in an attempt to get a cheap buzz, had eaten a mega-dose big enough to kill him, he would have discovered that fact a long time ago. I looked at Coke Bottle who continued squinting around the room as a look of panic emerged and spread across his face.

"I asked you why I shouldn't have done it," Coke Bottle snapped. "Why not?"

"Because that stuff can be deadly to humans," Josie said.

I knew immediately where Josie was going with the conversation and bit my lower lip to keep from laughing.

"Deadly?" Coke Bottle said. "Deadly how?"

"Really?" Josie said, raising an eyebrow in Coke Bottle's direction that I was sure he missed completely. "What part of deadly don't you understand?"

"Well, it sure didn't seem to bother me," Coke Bottle said.

"That's because it takes a while for the disease to kick in," Josie said.

"How long?"

"When did you take it?" Josie said.

Coke Bottle did the math silently in his head.

"Probably a couple of months ago," he said.

"Well, there you go," Josie deadpanned. "It usually takes around three months to take effect."

"What?" Coke Bottle said. "Did you hear that, Jerry?"

"Yeah, I heard her," Jerry said. "Don't worry about it."

"That's easy for you to say," Coke Bottle said. "You're not the one with a month to live."

Rooster shook his head and glanced at Josie who shrugged.

"What are the symptoms I should be on the lookout for?" Coke Bottle said.

"Will you just shut up?" Jerry snapped.

"Oh, don't worry," Josie said. "You'll know as soon as they hit. It's just a pity that it'll be too late by the time you start having those nasty seizures."

"You're cruel," I whispered, stifling another laugh.

"He's a dognapper," Josie whispered.

"Go easy on him. He's obviously not the sharpest tool in the shed," I said.

"Have you ever met anybody who ate dog sedatives to get high that was?" Josie said.

"Good point," I said.

"I can't believe I've only got a month to live," Coke Bottle said.

"Geez, enough," Rooster snapped. "She's just messing with your head, Walter. But if nothing happens to you in a month, give me a call, and I'll be happy to finish the job."

Coke Bottle got the message and fell silent. Rooster continued to stare down at both men who were unable to maintain eye contact.

"Tell you what, ladies," Rooster said. "Why don't you get ready to leave while I have a quiet word with my idiot brother and cousin?"

"We're just going to leave them here?" I said.

"Why not?" Rooster said. "They sure aren't going anywhere the way you've got them tied up. Jackson and the state police are on their way. Let them deal with them. I'd like to get you guys and your dog home safe and sound and then I'm going to take a very long nap."

Deciding that Rooster's logic was solid and since I was too tired to argue, I dragged myself toward the fireplace and began layering up for what promised to be a long, cold ride home. A few minutes later, we were ready to go, and I wrapped Dapper in a blanket and carried him outside. Apart from the straight-line track that Rooster's snowmobile had made on the way in, the entire landscape was an untouched thick blanket of white.

"Oh, my goodness," Chef Claire said, shielding her eyes from the glare cast by the rising sun. "It's the most beautiful thing I've ever seen."

"Chef Claire, as much as I hate to agree with anything you're saying at the moment, you're right," Josie said. "It's incredible."

I looked out over the horizon and nodded in agreement. The early morning sunlight caused the snow to shimmer and sparkle and, despite our recent ordeal and the aches and pains that coursed through my entire body, I felt strangely calm and at peace with the world.

This was the winter wonderland people wrote songs about.

Then a gust of wind kicked up, and a clump of swirling snow landed on my neck and started its slow, chilling slide down my back.

"Ah, crap," I said, grimacing.

"What is it?" Josie said, noticing my discomfort. "Full body cramp?"

"No, I got some snow down my back," I said.

"Oh, I hate when that happens," she said.

"Yeah, me too," I said. "Are you ready to go, Rooster?"

"Yup," he said, pointing at the boxy structure on skis that was attached to the back of his snowmobile. "Climb aboard."

"Okay. I guess I don't have a choice," I said as I tossed my skis in then climbed into the structure, groaning the entire time.

"Very ladylike," Josie deadpanned as I slid myself forward on my stomach. "If your mother could see you now."

"Let's see you do better," I said.

"Are you kidding?" Josie said. "I'll be lucky if I don't crack a rib getting into this thing.

I grabbed a thick blanket from the stack Rooster had brought with him and nestled up against the front of the structure blocking the wind the best I could.

"What is this thing?" I said.

"I use it to cart firewood in the winter," Rooster said. "I made it myself. I know it's not pretty to look at, but it'll do the trick."

"Rooster, right now, it looks like the Taj Mahal," I said.

He beamed at me and sat down on the snowmobile. Josie handed Dapper to me and then I slid over to make room for Josie and Chef Claire. We huddled close and hunched down as Rooster started the machine and slowly began our journey home. Despite its powerful engine, progress was slow as the machine struggled with the weight it was pulling over the thick, powdery snow.

A few minutes later I heard the unmistakable mouse-like crinkle. I glanced over at Josie who was munching on one of the bite-sized chocolate morsels.

"You want one?" she said, offering me the bag.

"Are they frozen?" I said, removing one of my gloves.

"No," she said. "But I'm sure they will be in a couple of minutes."

Chapter 17

Three hours later, all was again right with the world.

Rooster dropped off us off in front of the Inn after our one-hour journey home. We thanked him profusely before he roared away. Outside, the two-acre dog play area was being plowed and snowbanks that easily reached twenty feet were piled all over the place. Inside, Sammy and Jill had everything running like clockwork. They'd decided to not even bother trying to make the short trip back to their house, had raided our fridge at the house, and then spent the night in my office. We gave them the short version of our ordeal, got Dapper resettled into his condo, then said hello to all the dogs. And then the three of us headed up the already shoveled steps to the house, with Chloe and Captain leading the way.

"Man, that kid got here really early this morning," I said, amazed by the fact that our sidewalks and pathways were already snow-free. "I'm impressed."

"He's got the hots for Josie," Chef Claire said, laughing. "Maybe he thinks this will improve his chances."

"Perhaps in ten years if he learns how to cook and do laundry, who knows?" Josie said, chuckling.

"Speaking of cooking, who's up for some breakfast?" Chef Claire said.

"You read my mind."

After showers and a breakfast of macadamia nut pancakes and Canadian bacon, the three of us settled in front of the fire in our pajamas sipping hot chocolate and playing with the dogs. My phone

135

rang just as we were getting ready to start watching a movie. I recognized the number.

"Hey, Jackson," I said. "How's it going out there?"

"Delightful. At the moment, I'm walking through waist-deep snow and seriously considering a career change," he said. "But at least it's stopped snowing."

"Have you guys made it to Rooster's camp yet?"

"Yeah, we got here a couple of minutes ago," he said. "But I had to walk back outside to get cell reception."

"So you've met our captives," I said, laughing. "Aren't they a charming pair?"

"Uh, Suzy," Jackson said. "I hate to tell you this, but there's nobody here."

"What do you mean there's nobody there?" I said.

Josie and Chef Claire both looked at me. Josie motioned for me to put the phone on speaker. I did and then set the phone down on the coffee table.

"I'm surprised you didn't understand me. I thought I was perfectly clear," Jackson snapped.

"There's no need to get snarky, Jackson," I said.

"Oh, I don't know about that," Josie said. "Speaking from recent personal experience, I'd say he's got plenty to be snarky about."

"Thank you, Josie," Jackson said.

"You're welcome, Jackson," she said. "Let's see. There are the ten-foot snowdrifts. The wind-chill."

"Not to mention trying to walk through that chest-high snow," Chef Claire chimed in.

"Yeah, that was brutal," Josie said, nodding.

I glared at both of them.

"Are you two done?" I said, then refocused on the phone. "Well, if they aren't there, where on earth are they?"

"That is exactly the same question Detective Abrams and I were just discussing," Jackson said.

"Come on, Jackson," I said. "You're joking, right?"

"Does this sound like my joking voice, Suzy?"

"Well, they must have left some tracks when they managed to get away," I said.

"No, not a trace," Jackson said.

"They had a snowmobile in the shed near the house," I said. "That must have left a track."

"Nope," Jackson said.

"Maybe they just followed the same path that Rooster used when he came to get us. Did you check the track that Rooster's machine made to see if another snowmobile might have used it?"

"There's no need to do that," Jackson said.

"Jackson, you know how I hate to criticize your police work," I said.

"Yeah," Jackson deadpanned. "That's one of the things I've always loved about you, Suzy."

"Wow. You are in a mood," I said, shaking my head at the phone as my voice got louder. "Why on earth wouldn't you check that track to see if maybe another snowmobile used it?"

"Because their snowmobile is still in the storage shed," Jackson said.

"Oh," I whispered.

"Jackson one, Suzy zero," Chef Claire said, chuckling.

Josie snorted then took a sip of hot chocolate.

"Maybe a different snowmobile picked them up. Are you sure you don't see any other tracks?" I said.

"Yeah, I'm pretty sure about that," he said.

"Footprints?"

"No."

"Snowshoes?"

"Nope."

"Toboggan?"

"Toboggan? Really?" Jackson said, laughing. "I seriously doubt that they thought it would be a good day to go out and play in the snow, Suzy."

"How is this possible?" I said, glancing back and forth at Josie and Chef Claire.

"That's another great question Detective Abrams and I were just discussing."

"So what are you going to do?" I said.

"Probably keep scratching my head for a while," Jackson said. "Then we'll be talking with Rooster as soon as we get back. And we'll probably want to chat with the three of you at some point."

"Sure. We'll be here." I said.

"But right now, I'm making a bunch of calls to area hospitals, bars and restaurants, and all the other usual suspects to be on the lookout for them. I wish I had more to give them than just a general description. I called to let you know they're on the loose in case they decide to pay you guys another visit."

"I doubt if they're going to come back here," I said. "Did you know that one of the guys is Rooster's brother?"

"What? You mean, Jerry?" Jackson said.

"You know him?" I said.

"Yeah, we've met," Jackson said. "I thought he was dead."

"A couple of inches to the left and he might have been," Josie said.

I cringed at the memory of the sound the piece of firewood had made when it hit Jerry in the back of the head.

"What about the other guy?" Jackson said. "Did you find out who he was?"

"He's Rooster's cousin," I said. "At least that's what Rooster said."

"Big guy, who's blind as a bat without his glasses?" Jackson said.

"Yeah, that's him," I said. "Walter."

"Hmmm," Jackson said. "That's probably bad news."

"Why's that?"

"Because it means that they probably had help getting out of here," Jackson said. "Jerry and Walter could have trouble finding their way home from the next door neighbors."

"You don't think Rooster was the one who helped them escape, do you?" I said.

"When did he drop you guys off?" Jackson said.

"A couple of hours ago at least," I said.

"That's enough time," Jackson said. "Okay, that helps. I gotta run."

"Jackson, I don't think Rooster would have done that."

"Don't get me wrong, Suzy," Jackson said. "While I appreciate your input, I suggest you take the rest of the day off and stay out of it. And remember to keep an eye out just in case they decide to come back."

Jackson ended the call, and I sat back on the couch deep in thought as I rubbed Chloe's head.

"How on earth could anybody get out of that place without leaving a trail?" I said, eventually.

"Well," Josie said, finishing the last of her hot chocolate. "If they didn't go across the snow, then the only other option would have been from the air."

"Helicopter?" I said, frowning.

"It's a pretty remote area," Chef Claire said. "And I guess it's possible for a chopper to get in and out of there without being seen. There sure wouldn't have been many people outside at 5 AM."

"Apart from idiots like us," Josie said, glancing at Chef Claire. "By the way, thanks again for that."

"Will you please let it go?" Chef Claire said with a sigh.

"Maybe nobody saw it, but people would have heard it," I said, ignoring their ongoing battle about our ordeal Josie had nicknamed *Operation Whiteout*.

"Yeah, sure," Josie said. "But given the storm, most people probably would have just assumed it was doing some sort of search and rescue and not paid much attention to it. I know that's what I would have done."

"But who would have access to a helicopter?" I said. "Especially on such short notice."

"I don't know," Josie said. "But I'm willing to bet that it involves the mysterious *those people*."

"Which leads us back to the question of why someone wanted to steal Dapper in the first place," I said.

"Yeah," Josie said. "And the finger tattoo."

"You know what this means?" I said.

"That you're going to have to force yourself to have a date with the gorgeous guy from your mother's party?" Josie said.

"Yeah."

"Oh, no. Not the briar patch."

"Josie?"

"Yes, Suzy?" she said, laughing.

"Shut up."

Chapter 18

I stared out my office window and laughed as I watched Sammy hug himself for warmth and do his best to convince several dogs that they needed to follow him outside and take care of their business. Even though March had arrived, winter showed no signs of leaving, and it remained windy and cold. But at least it hadn't snowed since the storm, and people had gotten a bit of a reprieve and a chance to dig out.

I swiveled around in my chair, put my feet up on the desk and, for the third time, reviewed the list Josie and I had created that summarized what we knew about what we were now calling The Case of the Dapper Dandie Dinmont. And while we didn't know a lot, we certainly had more than enough questions to keep us busy.

First on our list was the question about who might have killed the guy Chef Claire had discovered under the ice. Josie and I had narrowed the suspects down. And when I say narrowed down, I mean that we no longer considered everyone walking around with a pulse a possible suspect. Since Millie, our friend who owned the Water's Edge, had seen the Baxter Brothers drinking with the victim, we had them near the top of the list. And while we refused to believe that Rooster was in any way involved, we had his brother and cousin on the list as well. The two dognappers were obviously followers, but history is littered with the bodies of people killed by others who, ostensibly, were merely following orders. And as to who might have given the order, also on our list were *those people*, an unknown entity that had the potential to expand our list of suspects until it, once again, included everyone walking around with a pulse.

By the time I finished my third review of our suspect list, I had realized I was merely repeating a futile, circular mental exercise that had given me a headache. I took some aspirin and stretched out on the couch with Chloe draped across my chest sound asleep. But as I closed my eyes hoping to join Chloe in a long, peaceful nap, I knew that the source of my headache was the very real possibility that William Wild, the man I'd be having dinner with tonight, was probably one of *those people.*

It would be just my luck that if the first man I'd been interested in a long time turned out to be a stone-cold killer.

Thankfully, before I could start obsessing over that possibility and ruining the rest of my morning, Josie came into my office and plopped down in a chair. She looked tired and like me was still feeling the aches and pains of our trek through the forest.

"What are you doing?" she said, reaching for the candy jar on the desk.

I gently slid Chloe to the other end of the couch before sitting up. Chloe stood, arched her back and yawned, then resettled in my lap.

"I was just doing some thinking," I said.

"How many times do I have to warn you about doing that?" she said, chuckling through a mouthful of chocolate. Then she nodded at my wrinkled clothes. "Did you sleep in those?"

"Yeah. I fell asleep on the couch, and when I woke up, I just came down here to start working on our list of suspects. My brain's been going in circles the past hour."

"I thought I smelled smoke."

"Funny. You got here just in time," I said, yawning. "I was just about to start calculating the probability that Just Call Me Bill is one of *those people.*"

"I wouldn't give it a lot of thought," Josie said, reaching into the candy jar again.

"Why not?" I said, grimacing as I tucked my legs underneath me.

"Because he is," Josie said, shrugging. "What we need to figure out is if his being one of *those people* is a bad thing."

"You know, that's a good point," I said.

"Thanks. You're welcome."

"We know that Rooster hates everything and everybody associated with the government and corporations. Maybe his warning about staying away from them was just part of his distrust and contempt for society in general."

"Do you really believe that?" Josie said.

I thought about it, then shook my head.

"No. But it sounded good when I thought of it," I said, laughing. "What am I going to do?"

"You're going to have dinner with him. Make small talk. Flirt with him for a while. Then maybe do some heavy snogging if the mood strikes," Josie said.

"Heavy snogging?" I said, frowning.

"It's a British term," Josie said, unwrapping a bite-sized Snickers. "It means to kiss amorously."

"Is that all?" I said.

"That's all the term means," Josie said, laughing. "But if you decide to take it further, I'm sure we can come up with a name for it." Then she turned serious and gave me her best deadpan look. "The things you're willing to do to solve a mystery. I gotta tell you, Suzy, it's inspirational."

"Shut up," I said, laughing. "The guy could be a killer."

144

"Yeah, I suppose he could be. Don't worry, your mother and Wentworth will be there, so I'm sure you'll be safe. And I imagine he has other things he'd like to do first before getting rid of you," she said, giving me an evil grin. "Besides, he could also just be an innocent bystander to whatever the heck is going on."

"I would hate to close that door now only to find out later that he's not involved," I said.

"That would be tragic," Josie said, putting her feet up on the desk.

"But if he is involved, I could end up dead," I said.

"Also tragic," Josie said.

"You know, you're really not helping, Josie."

"Disagree."

"Really?"

"I think I'm doing an excellent job of helping you sort through your options."

"Maybe. I have to admit that the heavy snogging option does sound interesting."

"Leave it to the British, huh?" she said.

A lightbulb went off in my head as a thought from my sub-conscious bubbled to the surface. Josie noticed the change in my expression and studied it for several moments for speaking.

"Well, I know you didn't leave the iron on. What is it?"

"It's probably nothing," I said, rubbing my forehead. "But you just mentioned the British."

"It's hard to work in a snogging reference without doing that," Josie said, sitting back in her chair to accommodate Chloe who'd woken up and decided she'd like to try out a fresh lap. "What about it?"

"I've spent hours trying to find a picture of the logo that was on the tee shirt the guy under the ice was wearing," I said. "I searched every sport, theater, and community activity I could think of in the States and Canada for various clubs. I've gone through literally thousands of pages of search results."

"Yeah, I know," Josie said. "And you came up empty. But like I told you the other day, there must be millions of different logos on tee shirts."

"But if it was from somewhere in the UK, it might not show up on any of my searches," I said, walking to the desk to turn on my laptop.

"Sure, it's possible," Josie said. "And didn't you say that Bill spent time working over there?"

"Yeah," I said, drumming my fingers on the desk. "I guess I should start with the most common sports."

"Sure, why not?" Josie said, shaking her head. "That should narrow it down to a couple hundred thousand possibilities."

"Can you think of a better idea?" I said.

"I guess you could try to identify every tee shirt company in the UK and send them a photo to see if they recognize the logo," Josie said.

"That would take forever. And there's no guarantee that all the companies even keep track of their previous orders. That tee shirt could have been made in someone's garage for all we know."

"Yeah, you're right," Josie said, nodding. "Okay, if you're determined to spend the rest of your day looking at logos, you might want to start your search with cricket and football."

"Football?" I said. "Oh, that's right, they call soccer football."

"Actually, I think it's the other way around, Suzy. We call football soccer."

"Tomato, tomahto," I said, typing various search words into my browser.

146

I clicked on the search button, and 1.3 seconds later, I blinked when I saw the number of returned results.

"How many possible hits did you get?" Josie said.

"Ten and a half million," I said, shaking my head.

"You might want to tighten up the search parameters a bit," she deadpanned.

"What would I do without you?" I said. "Thanks for the tip."

"You're welcome," Josie said, chuckling as she picked Chloe up off her lap then set her down on the couch. "As much as I'd love to stick around and watch you chase wild geese, I have a date with a gorgeous black Lab with a bad hip."

"Oh, the poor thing," I said, pausing to look up. "Is he going to be okay?"

"I think so, but I'll need to get some x-rays," Josie said. "He hurt it when he slipped on the ice. I'll catch you later, Google Meister."

I gave her a quick wave and refocused on my search. I knew what I was doing was a longshot, and I had no idea if I was even looking on the right continent. But since I was still waiting for Jackson to get back to me with the information about Jerry the Dognapper's phone records, I couldn't think of anything else to keep me busy, except accept Chef Claire's request to go cross-country skiing again.

Yeah, like that was gonna happen: There was a better chance I'd identify the source of the logo.

Fortunately, Chef Claire had caught Freddie on a light workday, and he'd quickly accepted her offer.

I kept refining my search parameters the best I could by breaking up the UK to individual countries and looking for local football clubs. I started with Wales and spent three hours scrolling through thousands of images displaying logos, badges, and other items but came up empty. I took a break for lunch and then resumed the same search using Scotland. Another three hours passed and I knew I would have to stop soon because of my dinner date with Bill.

And then on page eighty-seven of the search results, I stared at my screen wide-eyed with an open mouth.

"Unbelievable," I said to Chloe.

Chloe glanced up at me, wagged her tail, then closed her eyes and went back to sleep.

I texted Josie and a few minutes later she came in the office and stretched out on the couch. Chloe grudgingly made room for her.

"What's up?" Josie said.

"I found it," I said, beaming at her.

"Really? Well done," she said. "Where is it?"

"Scotland," I said. "Say, how's the Lab doing?"

"He's going to be fine," Josie said. "It's just a bone bruise. There's no sign of dysplasia."

"That's great news," I said.

"So where is it in Scotland?" Josie said, pulling a fresh bag of bite-sized Snickers out of her scrubs.

I waved her offer of the bag away and refocused on the image on my screen.

"I'm not sure," I said. "I texted you as soon as I found it."

Josie got up from the couch and stood behind me.

"Well, let's click the image and see what we find," she said.

"Please, please have the name of the town somewhere," I said, moving the mouse until the arrow was hovering over the image. I clicked the mouse, and the image expanded on my screen, and a small text box appeared underneath it.

"Alberfelderlyshire?" Josie said. "Man, that's a mouthful of town. Search for it."

I copied the text and clicked the search button. Several items came back, and I decided to start with what appeared to be the official town website.

"Alberfelderlyshire is a town of 300 residents nestled in the Scottish Highlands and founded in the early thirtieth century," I said, reading from the landing page. "Geez, that was a long time ago."

"Well, Europe is where all the history comes from," Josie said.

"Yeah, good point," I said, laughing.

"Kind of a long name for such a small town," Josie said. "What sort of links are there on the site?"

"Let's see," I said, scrolling down the page. "Churches, the local school, a couple of pubs, and, what do you know, the Alberfelderlyshire Football Club."

"Bingo," Josie said. "Click it."

I opened the site and in the top left corner of the page was a logo identical to the one on the dead man's tee shirt. I scrolled down until I saw a photo of the man identified as the president of the club. Next to the man's photo was a phone number.

"What time is it in Scotland?" I said.

"They're five hours ahead."

"Ten o'clock," I said. "A bit late, but probably not too bad, huh?"

"It's probably forgivable," Josie said. "Especially if we tell them anything they find interesting. Call the number."

I found the country code for Scotland, added it to the front of the phone number, and put the phone on speaker and dialed. A sleepy voice with a very thick Scottish accent answered on the fourth ring.

"Hello."

149

"Is this George McAllister?" I said.

"It is," he said. "And who might you be and why are you calling me at this hour?"

"I'm very sorry, sir," I said. "But I'm calling from the States, and I have a couple of questions about your football club."

"Okay," he said, obviously confused.

"Actually, it's about your club's logo," I said, a bit unsure about how to get the conversation rolling.

"Our logo?" the man said, then let loose with a sleepy half-grumble, half-cackle laugh. "Oh, I get it now. Okay, Gertie, do you mind telling me why you're calling in the middle of the night to pull my leg?"

"No, sir," I said. "My name is Suzy Chandler, and I'm really calling from the States. Your club's logo was on the tee shirt of a man we found recently under the ice."

"Dead?"

"Very," I said.

Josie snorted.

"He was wearing a tee shirt over there in February?" the man said. "I'm not much on Yank geography, but that sounds a wee bit peculiar."

"Yes, it is," I said. "It's a long story."

"All the good ones are, lass," he said, chuckling.

I decided I liked Mr. McAllister.

"But the man didn't have any identification on him and nobody seems to know who he was," I said. "And the logo was the only thing we had to go on. So when we finally figured out it was the logo for your football club, I thought it might be worth a phone call. And I'm really sorry to call you this late in the evening."

"Pay it no mind," he said.

"So we were wondering if you might know of any unsolved missing person reports in your town," I said.

We waited out several seconds of silence before he responded.

"No, I don't think so," he said. "It's a very small town, and that would have been very big news. But I guess someone could have gone missing up at the orphanage."

"Orphanage?" I said, raising an eyebrow at Josie.

"Yes. There's an orphanage just outside of town that's run by a religious group. We see the kids and the people who run the place around town sometimes, but they generally keep to themselves. I guess it's possible that one of them took off and disappeared but we would never know about it. They're a pretty secretive bunch."

"I don't see anything on your website about the orphanage," I said, scrolling up and down the landing page.

"Hah," he said, laughing. "You won't find anything about them anywhere. Trust me, I've looked. Like I said, they're very secretive and keep to themselves."

"Interesting," I said. "Is there anything else you can tell us?"

"Other than the fact that we haven't won a match yet this year, not much," he said.

"Well, I appreciate your time, Mr. McAllister," I said.

"My pleasure, lass. If you have a photo of the man in the tee shirt, I'd be happy to take a look at it."

"That would be great, sir. Thank you."

"My email address is on our site. Just shoot it over, and I'll let you know if I recognize him."

"I'd really appreciate it," I said, reaching for my phone.

"Good luck with your search," he said. "And I wish I had more I could tell you. But we're a sleepy little town, and not much happens around here that would make the news."

Now that he was waking up, it was quickly becoming apparent that Mr. McAllister was a bit of a chatterbox.

"I understand completely," I said, preparing to hang up.

"Yeah, it's pretty quiet around here. And that's just the way we like it. In fact, apart from the dang dog that disappeared, I can't think of a single thing out of the ordinary that's happened here in the last year."

Josie and I stared at each other dumbfounded. I set my phone back down on the desk.

"No way," Josie whispered.

"Uh, Mr. McAllister? Did you say that a dog disappeared?" I said, staring down at the phone.

"Yeah, and not just a dog. A pretty famous dog. At least around these parts," he said.

"It wasn't a Dandie Dinmont by any chance was it?" I said.

We heard him gasp on the other end of the line.

"How did you know that?" he said.

"Because I think we might have him," I said.

"In the States?"

"Yeah."

"Well, I'll be," he said. "Then you'll need to speak with Mrs. Angus straight away. You got something to write with?"

"Go ahead," I said, grabbing a pen and scribbling down the phone number. "Thanks so much, sir. We'll let you know how it all turns out."

"No need for that, lass," he said, laughing. "I'm sure I'll hear all about it. But feel free to call anytime. And don't forget to send me that photo."

"It's already on its way," I said.

"Really? Then hang on a minute," he said. "Let me check my email."

"This is incredible," Josie said. "You've outdone yourself this time, Suzy."

"Thanks," I said, exhaling loudly. "We got lucky."

"It's more than luck, and you know it," Josie said. "But it opens up a whole bunch of new questions."

"Yeah, it certainly does," I said.

"Okay, I got it," Mr. McAllister said when he returned to the phone. "It's definitely one of our tee shirts, but I'm afraid I don't recognize the man in the picture."

"Thanks again, sir," I said.

"No problem. Now promise me you'll call Mrs. Angus right away. She's been at her wit's end for months."

"I guarantee we'll be calling her as soon as we get off the phone with you, sir."

"Then I'll say goodnight."

"Goodnight, Mr. McAllister."

I hung up and immediately dialed the woman's number. She answered on the first ring.

"Are you the woman calling from the States?" she whispered excitedly into the phone.

"Wow. Word travels fast over there," Josie said, laughing.

"Yes, my name is Suzy Chandler. How did you know that?" I said, frowning.

153

"Mac sent me a message a few minutes ago telling me that he was on the phone with somebody who had found Lancelot," she said, the hope in her voice unmistakable.

"Lancelot," I said.

"Cool name," Josie said.

"Is he okay?" Mrs. Angus said.

"He's fine," I said, then caught the look Josie was giving me. I got the point and nodded. "Apart from how much he's missing you, of course."

Then Mrs. Angus broke down and started sobbing uncontrollably. We waited it out, then continued.

"Can you give us a minute, Mrs. Angus?" I said. "We just need to check something before we continue."

"You're going to see how he responds to his name, aren't you?" she said.

"Yes, we are, Mrs. Angus," I said, standing up.

"Are you a dog person?"

"Yes, very much so," I said. "Hang in there. I'll be right back.

Josie and I headed straight for Dapper's condo. He woke up when he heard us, then sat staring at us about ten feet away from the condo door.

"Lancelot. Come here, boy. Come here, Lancelot," Josie said.

The dog raced to the door and hopped excitedly on his back legs. He barked loudly, which started an extended round of barking from many of our other guests before it quieted down. Lancelot continued to hop up and down and lick Josie's hand.

Josie and I both lost it and our eyes filled with tears.

"This should be a happy time," I said, wiping my eyes with my sleeve.

154

"It is," Josie said. "It's just emotional. Look at him. It's like he's realized that somebody has actually figured out who he is."

"Let's bring him with us," I said, opening the condo door.

Josie scooped him up in her arms, and we headed back to my office. She put the dog on top of the desk near the phone.

"Mrs. Angus?"

"Yes," she said.

At the sound of her voice, Lancelot cocked his head and stood still.

"It's him," I said. "Can you say something so he can hear your voice?"

"Lancelot. Who's the good boy?" she cooed.

The dog began barking and started doing wheelies on top of the desk. We couldn't help laughing and waited until Lancelot wore himself out. He sat down and stared intensely at the phone.

"Somebody's pretty excited over here at the moment," I said.

"Somebody is pretty excited over here, too."

"I guess you'll need some directions to get here," I said.

"Yes, please," Mrs. Angus said. "I'll be on the first flight I can find."

"You'll want to fly into either Syracuse or Ottawa," I said.

"I should fly into either the States or Canada?" she said.

"We're right on the border," I said. "You'll understand when you see the place."

"I can probably get there by tomorrow evening," she said. "Is that okay?"

"That's fine, Mrs. Angus," I said. "And we'd be honored if you'd spend the night with us."

"And you'll have Lancelot with you when I get there?"

155

"Don't worry, Mrs. Angus," I said. "I don't think we could stop him even if we wanted. We'll see you tomorrow."

"I can't thank you enough," she said, again breaking down.

"We're just glad we were able to reconnect you two," I said. "And I'm sure we'll have lots to talk about. Okay, you should probably go get some sleep."

"No chance of that happening," she said, laughing. "Good night, Lancelot. Mumsy will see you tomorrow."

I ended the call then stroked Lancelot's head. Still excited and more than a little bit confused, the dog sat down on the desk and glanced back and forth at us.

"Mumsy?" Josie said. "Must be a British thing."

"She's Scottish," I said, laughing.

"Close enough," Josie said.

"I think I've heard enough British terms for one day," I said, glancing up at the clock.

"That's right. You've got to get ready for a night of heavy snogging."

"Shut up," I said, punching her on the arm on my way to the door. "You got everything under control here?"

"Yeah, I'm good," Josie said, reaching for a bite-sized Snickers. "You go shower and snog away."

"Snog away? Is that more British slang?"

"No, that one's all mine."

"Not one of your better efforts," I said, exiting the office.

"Disagree."

Her laughter followed me all the way down the hall.

Chapter 19

I knocked on my mother's front door and let myself in. I hung my coat on the rack near the door and removed my shoes then slid my feet into a pair of the Japanese slippers my mother had organized by size in a row along one wall. She'd never allowed shoes in the house and, as a child, I'd gotten used to going barefoot in the summer, and wearing thick wool socks the rest of the year. But a couple of years ago, my mother had taken a trip to Japan and fallen in love with the idea of slippers being worn around the house. She told everyone that she was simply tired of looking at other people's ugly feet, but I knew the real reason was that it added one more quirk to the list of things that enhanced her reputation as one of our more *colorful* local residents.

When I'd protested, she had threatened to add kimonos to the mix, so I quickly decided it was easier to just shut up and wear the slippers.

As far as this evening's attire went, I'd gone with a loose-fitting cashmere sweater my mother had given me for Christmas and a pair of jeans that were well-worn, but not yet ragged. Just before I left the house, Josie and Chef Claire had both paused to look up from their Thai chicken curry and nod their approval at my outfit. Then Josie had laughingly called it; snog-appropriate. I punched her on the arm on my way out the door, and their laughter continued until I reached my SUV and was finally out of earshot. I knew the banter was good-natured and that they hoped my date went well, but my brief interaction with them had only added to my nervousness.

I rarely got nervous about dates because I had two cardinal rules I stuck with. The first was to keep my expectations extremely low. That minimized the potential for crushing disappointment while still offering me the chance to be truly surprised and delighted should things go well. The second cardinal rule was to maintain self-control at all times and react swiftly should my date say or do anything in an attempt to shift the balance of power unfairly in their direction.

Josie and I had discussed my dating philosophy many times, more frequently of late, since it was becoming obvious that something wasn't working. One of the men my mother had fixed me up a few months ago had remarked that being on a date with me reminded him of a boxing match where the two fighters spent the first couple of rounds feeling each other out as they tried to identify their opponent's weaknesses. Normally I would have applauded his insight and probably agreed to a second dinner date, but he'd offered his observation while his hand was under my dress and working its way up my thigh under the table. With a soft whisper in his ear about sending him back to his corner in search of his cut man, I also informed him that I wasn't above punching below the belt. The hand, along with the rest of him, soon disappeared.

I liked to think that tonight wouldn't be any different. Should the need arise, my second cardinal rule would kick in, and I'd be able to maintain a level playing field. But Bill Wild had gotten under my skin. I continued to hope that my interest in him was solely related to discovering what, if any, role he'd had in the murder of the man under the ice as well as identifying the significance of the elaborate finger tattoo both men had.

Who am I trying to kid? And why was I lying to myself?

I'd spent about a minute deciding on the jeans and cashmere sweater, but ten minutes deciding what to wear underneath them. Anytime I did that I knew my cardinal rules were malfunctioning and that my mind definitely wasn't focused on solving a murder. The best I could hope for was that he would do something stupid, like lie to me again, or I could be facing the very real possibility of being a willing participant in a multi-round clench with no referee in sight to break it up.

As I walked toward the entertainment room, I had to give my mother her due; the slippers felt great. I found her and Bill sitting on one of the couches sipping wine and chatting. They both looked up when I entered, and Bill stood to greet me. He extended his hand, pulled me in for a hug and gave me a peck on the cheek.

"Hi, stranger," he said, beaming at me. "You look fantastic."

"Thanks, I said, feeling my face flush. "Good to see you, Bill. Hi, Mom."

"Hello, darling," she said, accepting my hug while still seated on the couch. "Have a seat, and I'll pour you a glass of wine."

I sat down across from them, watched her pour, then took a sip of wine.

"Where's Wentworth?" I said, glancing at a new piece of artwork hanging above the fireplace.

"He's in the kitchen, darling. He insisted on doing all the cooking tonight."

"You got him trained early, Mom," I said, giving her a smile as I looked at her over the top of my wine glass.

"Funny, darling," she said. "But let's not start with that, okay?"

I nodded and took another sip of wine.

"You look fantastic, darling," she said, nodding her approval. "Doesn't she look great, Bill?"

"Absolutely," he said, giving me a big smile. "Very snoggable."

My mother laughed as she got up and headed toward the kitchen.

"Let me go check with Wentworth to see how dinner is coming along."

"I beg your pardon?" I said after she'd left the room.

"What? Snoggable? It's a British term for-"

"I know what it means," I said, taking a gulp of wine. "So you think I'm what, snog-worthy?"

He sat upright and appeared confused. Then he softened, and his smile returned.

"Why, yes," he said. "I certainly do."

Nervous energy flooded through me, and I drained the rest of my wine. I glanced at the kitchen, then did something I'd never done in my life. And when I say it's something I've never done, I mean that I've never done it at the start of a first date. And I'd most certainly had never done it with my mother in the next room.

I climbed onto his lap, pushed his head back until it rested on the back of the couch, and kissed him. The kiss started slow, then turned hard and deep and seemed to last forever. Then I pulled away, exhaled loudly, and sat back down in my chair across from him.

"Okay, I'm good. That'll get me through dinner," I said.

"What was that?" Bill said, reaching for his wine glass.

"Isn't that what's called a snog?" I said, trying to deal with a host of emotions that ran the gamut from unbridled lust to intense embarrassment.

"It certainly is," he said, laughing. "But what on earth possessed you to do that? Not that I'm complaining."

"I guess it was something I just needed to do. You know, get it over with," I said, my face flushed red.

"Get it over with?" he said, still laughing. "How romantic."

"Yeah, well it's the best I can come up with on short notice," I said, again exhaling loudly. "Wow. That was a good kiss."

"Yes," Bill said. "And I hope it's not the last one of the evening."

"I guess that's going to depend," I said, gradually recovering my composure.

"On what?"

"Probably on a lot of things," I said, glancing at the kitchen. "I wonder what's keeping dinner."

"Are you all right, Suzy?" he said, leaning forward.

"There are a lot of theories floating around about that question," I said, refilling my wine glass.

For some reason, he found my comment funny and he laughed long and hard. I forced myself to remain in my seat and hoped that my mother returned soon. If not, there was a good chance we'd all be highly embarrassed even before the salad was served. I spent the next several minutes staring off into space, punctuating my feigned disinterest with sips of wine and the occasional sneak peek at him.

Eventually, my mother called us into the dining room. Bill stood and waited for me to go first, then placed a hand on my lower back as I walked past him. I felt my body twitch, and I picked up the pace and sat down at the table.

"Hi, Suzy," Wentworth said as he entered the dining room carrying a large covered serving dish.

"Hey, Wentworth," I said smiling at him. "Thanks for inviting me."

"My pleasure," he said, removing the top on the dish. "I just hope my cooking skills do the recipe justice.

A flood of familiar smells filled the table.

161

"That's Chef Claire's beef bourguignon, isn't it?" I said, delighted to have something to focus on other than my attack on Bill in the other room.

"It is indeed," he said, filling my plate with noodles then ladling a generous portion of the beef dish over the top.

I waited until we were all served, participated in the toast my mother offered, felt Bill's hand on my thigh, and then started eating. Fortunately, the food was so good, Bill decided he needed both hands to eat, and he released his grip.

Maybe a relationship, as Josie had suggested, was central to my eating less. As I snuck covert glances at him during dinner, I thought there might be a possibility I'd be less obsessed with food if he were around on a regular basis. Then I got a forkful of the beef, along with a pearl onion and a slice of porcini, and reconsidered. It wasn't as good as Chef Claire's version, but it was delicious. And when I didn't hesitate to accept Wentworth's offer of seconds, I smiled when the self-bestowed moniker surfaced from my subconscious.

I continued to smile and nod my head until I caught my mother staring at me across the table. I shrugged, hid the smile, and slurped a mouthful of noodles down.

Yes, I decided. It was a term I could live with, even wear with pride.

I was officially a food-snogger.

"Penny for your thoughts, darling," my mother said, taking a sip of champagne that probably cost more than my car.

"I'd hate to see you overpay, Mom," I said, laughing. "I was just sitting here thinking about my relationship with food."

"Oh, let's not go there, darling. Tell us all about your recent adventure in the woods."

162

"Adventure?" Bill said, looking at me. "I love adventures. Do tell."

"My daughter and her friends got lost in the woods during the blizzard the other day."

"Really?" Bill said. "That sounds dangerous."

"Especially when dealing with two hardened criminals," my mother said.

"What?" Bill said, glancing back and forth at us.

"Tell the story, darling."

My mother sat back in her chair, wiped her mouth, and waited.

So I told the story, beginning with our ill-fated attempt at cross-country skiing. Bill listened carefully, laughed at the appropriate times, and demonstrated the perfect amount of sympathy. When I got to the part about how Chef Claire had taken one of the men down with the ball of ice, everyone roared with laughter.

"I wish I could have seen that," Bill said, still chuckling as he grabbed his glass of champagne.

"Yeah, Coke Bottle didn't know what hit him," I said, smiling.

"What?" Bill said, frowning. "Coke Bottle?"

"It's the nickname we gave him because he wore really thick glasses," I said.

"Oh, I see," Bill said, breaking eye contact, then recovering almost immediately.

"So what on earth were those two doing out in the woods?" Bill said.

"They were hiding a dog they'd stolen from the Inn," I said.

"A dog?" Bill said.

I watched him fold his hands together before placing his elbows on the table. I decided it was subconscious, but he'd put his hands

163

together in a way that hid his finger tattoo. I studied him for a moment, before continuing. Since it was one of the topics that needed to be dealt with before Bill and I went any further, I decided to just put it out there.

"Yes," I said. "For some reason, they felt compelled to steal him. A Dandie Dinmont. There are some truly despicable people out there."

Bill visibly flinched, and my heart sank.

"Despicable," Wentworth said, refilling everyone's glass. "But it sounds like everything worked out well in the end."

"Yes, I guess it did," I said, glancing at Bill who was sipping his champagne with a blank stare on his face.

I decided not to reveal the fact that we'd reconnected Lancelot with his owner and that she would be arriving sometime tomorrow.

"Okay, if we're done with that discussion," my mother said. "I'd like to propose a new topic. Ice fishing."

I groaned, and Wentworth exhaled audibly.

"Geez, Mom. I don't know. I'm pretty busy at the moment."

"Darling, you and I both know that's a complete line of bull," she said, wagging a finger at me. "Part of our tradition is that we always go ice fishing at least one time each winter. And you've been ducking it so far this year. Besides, Wentworth has never been ice fishing, and I know he's dying to give it a shot. Aren't you, sweetheart?"

"Yes, Snuggles," Wentworth said.

I fought back a laugh. It was obvious that Wentworth wanted to go ice fishing about as much as he had wanted to ride on the back of my mother's snowmobile.

"Then that settles it," my mother said. "Saturday. We'll meet here at seven in the morning."

"Geez, Mom."

"Don't whine, darling. It's not ladylike," she said. "We need to get out there before the ice melts."

"Where's global warming when you need it?" I whispered.

Wentworth heard it and snorted.

"Did you say something, darling?"

"No, Mom."

"Good. So what's the plan?" she said, staring at me.

"Saturday. Seven in the morning," I said, beaten.

"That's my girl," she said. "And bring Josie and Chef Claire. How about you, Bill? Feel like going out in ten-degree weather to do battle with a Northern Pike through a sheet of ice?"

"Gee, it sounds great," he said.

"Liar," I whispered.

My comment got another laugh out of Wentworth, but my mother cut it short with a glare.

"I'm sorry, Mrs. C.," Bill said, glancing at Wentworth. "But I'm afraid work is going to have come first. I have some things to take care of back in New York."

"The world of high finance never sleeps, right?" Wentworth said. "Thanks again for handling that one. I should probably be doing it myself."

"But you can't because you're going ice fishing, right?" my mother said, smiling at Wentworth.

"Yes, Snuggles," he whispered as he took a big gulp of champagne.

"There you go," my mother said, patting him on the forearm before turning back to Bill. "Maybe next time."

"I look forward to it," Bill said, then glanced down at his phone that was buzzing. "I'm sorry, but we should take this one. It's Jerome."

165

Wentworth nodded, and he and Bill walked into the entertainment room.

"Well, darling," my mother said. "What do you think?"

"It was good, but it just didn't have Chef Claire's magic touch," I said, taking a sip of champagne.

"Funny, darling," she said, waiting for my response.

"He's gorgeous," I said.

"Yes, he is," she said.

"But there's something about him that bothers me," I said.

"Yes. Me too."

"Really?"

"Yeah," my mother said, swirling the champagne in her glass and studying the bubbles. "At first I thought it was just because of what he does for a living. Finance guys aren't usually the most exciting creatures walking around."

"Like Wentworth, for example?" I said, raising an eyebrow at her.

"Exactly," she said, then leaned forward and whispered. "What sort of man won't even take his socks off in bed?"

"Then why are you keeping him around?" I said.

"Maybe because he's a nice man and I don't want to hurt his feelings?" she said.

"Really, Mom?" I said, laughing. "I don't remember that ever being high on your list of concerns before."

"There's a lot you don't know, darling," she said, topping off our glasses. "But I take your point. He's getting very fond of me, and I need to make sure Wentworth has the opportunity to *see all sides of me* before it gets to the point where it will be even harder to extricate myself."

"You mean by doing things like taking him ice fishing?" I said, grinning as the lightbulb came on.

"Yes," she said, flashing me a coy smile. "I'm not being very brave about this am I?"

I laughed and shook my head.

"Mom, you are one for the books," I said.

"I guess I have my moments," she said, shrugging. "So, getting back to Bill."

"I don't know about you, Mom, finance guys usually might be pretty boring, but I think he's very exciting."

"Yes, he certainly is," she said. "But there's something that really bothers me about him. And it's driving me crazy because I don't know what it is."

"Well, for one, he's a liar," I said.

"Yes, I'm sure he is," she said, sighing. "I need to slow down. This champagne is going to my head."

"Are you planning on driving later?"

"No."

"Then you should give yourself permission to cut loose a bit," I said.

"Thank you, darling," she said, taking another sip. "But a man who tells the occasional lie certainly isn't unique by any means."

"No, it's not," I said.

"And probably not enough to keep him off the catch and release list," she said, giving me an evil grin.

"I'm not sure about that," I said.

It was true. I wasn't.

"I bet he's a lot of fun," she said, grinning at me over the top of her glass.

167

"I have no doubt about it, Mom."

That was also true. I didn't.

"So what are you going to do?" she said.

I thought about her question.

"Well, I'm going to sit here chatting with you over dessert and coffee and wait until this champagne buzz subsides. Then I'm going to go home, and debrief the evening with Josie while curled up on the couch with the dogs."

"What would you do without Josie and your dogs?"

"I can't even fathom that, Mom," I said.

Also true. I couldn't.

"And that's exactly what you need to find with a man, darling."

"I know that, Mom."

"But that doesn't mean you can't have some fun while you're looking for him," she said, laughing.

Maybe it was the champagne or the fact that I was tired of thinking about my lack of a relationship. Whatever the reason was, I laughed along with my mother and then we clinked glasses, toasting each other's lifestyle choices.

"It sounds like you two are having a lot of fun," Wentworth said, sitting back down at the table. "What did I miss?"

"Oh, we were just discussing the merits of the catch and release program," my mother said.

"A discussion about fishing?" he said, frowning.

"Yes, sweetheart," my mother said. "Something like that."

"Sorry I missed that one," he said.

"Liar," I whispered.

He laughed and raised his glass to me in salute.

"Bill needs to run, but he'd like to say goodbye before he goes," Wentworth said.

"Of course," I said, standing up. "Excuse me for a moment. I'll be right back."

"Take all the time you need, darling."

I headed toward the front door and found Bill removing his slippers and putting his boots back on.

"I hear you have to run," I said, definitely feeling the effects of the champagne.

"Sorry, but duty calls," he said. "I was looking forward to seeing more of you tonight."

"I bet you were," I said, laughing.

"Maybe next time," he said, grabbing his jacket.

I removed the jacket from his hand and set it aside, then moved in for another long, deep kiss. I eventually broke away and smiled at him.

"Yeah, maybe next time," I said.

"Do you mean that?" he said.

"Maybe."

"If I can get back up here next week, are you interested in making a night of it?"

"Maybe."

"You seem to have some doubts," he said, putting his jacket on.

"You can be sure of that," I said.

"Okay," he said. "But the kiss was good, right?"

"Maybe," I said with a smile.

"Goodnight, Suzy," he said, laughing as he waved and went out the door.

I watched through one of the windows near the door as he made his way to his car and drove away.

I glanced at myself in the hallway mirror.

"Wow," I whispered. "You dodged a bullet tonight, girl."

Chapter 20

Mrs. Fenella Angus was an attractive woman we guessed was somewhere in her fifties, intelligent, and had recently become a widow. She had a salt and pepper perm, a bubbly personality, and an accent thicker than one of Chef Claire's sandwiches. I was sure she assumed that the rapt attention Josie and I were paying to her lengthy tale about Lancelot's disappearance and the impact it had on her life was because we found the story fascinating. While the story was interesting, we were on the edge of our seats listening closely to everything she said because there were times when we couldn't understand a word she was saying.

When she arrived, we had Lancelot ready to go. We'd given him a bath, groomed him meticulously, and then wrapped a new tartan scarf around his neck. He seemed to realize that something good was about to happen, and when we brought him up to the house in the afternoon to wait for his owner's arrival, he paced back and forth and roamed the house to help kill time. Upon seeing her standing in the doorway, Lancelot had jumped into her arms and let loose with several rounds of whimpers and yips that brought tears to our eyes and reconfirmed we'd gone into the right business. Mrs. Angus eventually stopped crying and was able to resume normal breathing after Josie had poured her what Mrs. Angus referred to as a *wee spot of sherry*. As she continued to tell her story, Lancelot remained draped across her chest and seemed to be hugging her.

She lovingly stroked the dog's head as she listened to us recount Lancelot's ordeal and our subsequent rescue efforts in the blizzard.

When we finished, all three of us fell silent and waited for the first question to come up. Mrs. Angus went first.

"Do you have any idea why those men would want to steal Lancelot?" she said, nuzzling the dog.

"We were about to ask you the same question, Mrs. Angus," Josie said.

"Please, call me Fenella," she said. "Well, Lancelot is rated as the top male Dandie in Scotland. So I assume he was stolen for the purposes of breeding."

"That makes sense I guess," Josie said.

"Perhaps, but the Dandie population is so small, and there aren't that many breeders. And we're a very close-knit community. If someone had tried to register a litter of puppies, the lineage on the papers would have led straight back to Lancelot. And, of course, to me."

"What if someone wanted to breed the dogs for another reason?" Josie said.

"Like what?" Fenella said.

"Probably a puppy mill," I said.

Fenella Angus's face morphed into a ferocious snarl, and she hugged Lancelot even tighter.

"I'd like to get my hands on them," she said.

"So would we," Josie said.

I paused as Chef Claire entered carrying a tray of warm crumpets, assorted jams, and an Amaretto cream sauce Josie and I were very familiar with.

"Oh, my," Fenella said, recognizing the crumpets immediately. "My dear, you shouldn't have gone to all that trouble. Look at that, they're still warm."

172

"No trouble at all, Mrs. Angus," Chef Claire said. "And I know the cream sauce isn't very traditional, but please give it a try. I think you'll like it."

"Listen to her, Fenella," Josie said, closely eyeing the tray.

"In case you're having trouble with the math, there's a dozen," I said, laughing.

"I can count, thank you very much," Josie said, piling a healthy serving of raspberry jam on a crumpet and topping it with a thick layer of the cream sauce.

"Oh, my goodness," Fenella said, staring up at Chef Claire. "These are wonderful."

"Thank you," Chef Claire said, beaming.

"Where on earth did you come up with the idea to serve crumpets?" Fenella said.

"We wanted to do something that would remind you of home," Chef Claire said. "And it was either these or serve haggis for dinner," Chef Claire said.

Josie and I both laughed.

"We're sorry, Fenella," Josie said. "But heart, liver, and lungs stuffed into a sheep's stomach didn't stand a chance against these babies."

"Good call," Fenella said, swallowing the last bite of her first crumpet. "My dear, are you sure you don't have a wee bit of Scottish blood in you?"

Chef Claire laughed and waved as she headed back into the kitchen.

"Is everything she cooks as good as these?" Fenella said.

"Oh, yeah," Josie said, assembling another crumpet.

"Even better," I said. "I think this is the first time she's ever made these."

"You are two lucky ladies," Fenella said.

"Indeed we are, Fenella," I said, then caught a glimpse of the mess Josie was making. "Geez, Josie. Try taking human bites."

"Reuniting dogs with their owners always makes me hungry," she said, shrugging.

I shook my head and forced myself to get my mind off the crumpets.

"So you really don't have any idea who took Lancelot in the first place?" I said.

"No," she said. "I can't think of anyone in town who would do something like that. But I certainly wouldn't put it past someone from that orphanage."

"Mr. McAllister mentioned it over the phone. He said it's run by a religious organization," I said.

"Hah," Fenella scoffed. "Religious organization my left foot. All you need to do is take a look at some of the people that live there, and it will quickly become clear that orphanage isn't affiliated with any church I'm familiar with."

"Mr. McAllister said they were mysterious and pretty much kept to themselves," I said.

"Yes," Fenella said, chuckling. "I always thought that was one of their better qualities."

"Don't be shy," I said, noticing her glancing at the rapidly dwindling stack of crumpets. "Have another."

"I probably shouldn't," she said, reaching for one. "But if I'm going to, I guess I shouldn't wait too long."

"Don't worry, Fenella," I said, glancing at Josie. "As long as you don't try to take the last one, you'll be safe."

"Funny," Josie said through a mouthful of cream sauce.

"Would you mind taking a look at a couple of pictures to see if you recognize the man found under the ice?" I said, reaching for the photos.

"Not at all," she said, wiping her hands with a napkin.

I handed her one of the photos.

"Yes," she said almost immediately. "He was definitely from the orphanage."

"Do you know his name?" I said.

"No," she said, shaking her head. "I never spoke with him, but he seemed to be one of the more normal residents."

"Normal in what way?" I said.

"He was part of a small group that hung around town from time to time and was the only one who seemed to make an effort to smile and be polite."

"It seems odd that in a town as small as yours that you wouldn't have spoken to him at some point," I said.

"It is odd," she said. "But the townspeople and the orphanage have developed a hands-off policy with each other over the years. They pride themselves on being self-sufficient and, while we residents consider ourselves a friendly lot, we can be quite insular when it comes to outsiders."

"But you're sure he came from the orphanage?" I said.

"Without a doubt, my dear," she said, nodding.

"Okay," I said, handing her a close-up photo of the finger tattoo.

Fenella blanched when she saw it, blinked several times, then stared at me.

175

"Where on earth did you get this?" she said.

"It's a tattoo that was on the victim's index finger," I said. "Do you recognize it?"

"Yes, I'm afraid I do," she whispered. "Oh, my."

"What is it?" I said.

"It's one of the symbols used to identify the members of an ancient secret society," she said.

"What?" I said, staring at her.

"Yes. At least that's how it was told to me when I was growing up. I've always thought all the stories about *those people* were, pardon the expression, old wives' tales and just part of some mythology used to get children to eat their vegetables and keep them in line."

Yet another reference to *those people*. If I didn't get some clarification soon about who these people were, I was going to get cranky.

"I'm sorry, Fenella," Josie said. "But I'm confused."

"Yes, as am I, my dear."

"But what's the connection to the Dandie Dinmont?" I said.

"According to the legend, centuries ago, the Dandie was selected to represent this secret group for several reasons that match the qualities expected of society members," Fenella said.

"Centuries ago?" I said.

"Yes," she said.

"These people must be really good at keeping secrets," Josie said.

"Indeed," Fenella said, nodding at Josie before continuing. "As I'm sure you know after spending so much time with Lancelot, the Dandie is extremely intelligent but very independent."

We both nodded in agreement.

"And while they like to relax when they're around the people they're closest to, they are brave and tenacious when threatened or when their hunting instincts kick in," Fenella said, gently rubbing Lancelot's generous tuft of hair on the top of his head. "They also have a quiet confidence and don't go in for a lot of *macho* behaviors. As such, they can be quite the diplomat when necessary, but yet they're assertive when the situation calls for it. They have a mind of their own and, as such, need to be consistently led in the direction you want them to go. And to complicate things even further, since they can be sensitive and very proud, if you get too heavy-handed with them, they can become most uncooperative." She tousled the dog's hair. "Can't you, Lancelot?"

The dog barked loudly once before burying his head under her arm.

"That sounds like a list of characteristics you'd expect from a soldier," Josie said.

"Indeed," Fenella said.

"Or a corporate executive," I said, glancing at Josie, but thinking about Bill.

"I had no idea that the society might be real," Fenella said.

"Or that it could have a connection with the orphanage," I said.

"Indeed. I imagine putting an orphanage in a remote location where the locals would pretty much ignore everyone who lives there does make some sense," Fenella said.

"But what does this secret society actually do?" Josie said.

"According to the legend, their mission is to train what they call *Meesun-Mercens*. It's a combination of a missionary and mercenary. And once they're trained, they are deployed to infiltrate."

"Infiltrate what?" I said, frowning.

177

"Everything," Fenella said. "Schools and universities, business and government, you name it."

"And do what?" Josie said.

"Promote the philosophy and interests of *Comann*. It's a Gaelic term that means community, or society," Fanella said, staring off into the distance. "And all this time, we always thought it was akin to Aesop's Fables." She glanced back and forth at us. "Their foot soldiers are supposedly identified by a crescent-shaped tattoo on their back."

"Something like this?" I said, handing her another photo.

"Yes," she whispered. "Exactly."

"Do you know anything about the significance of the Dandie tattoo?" I said.

"Again, this is all part of the legend," she said. "Or at least what I thought was a legend. The tattoo of the Dandie is reserved for the elite members of Comann. I can't remember what they need to do to earn it, but it's obviously related to the breed's qualities we talked about earlier."

"I need to call Wentworth," I said.

"Yes, you do," Josie said.

"How do I go about telling my mother's boyfriend that one of his most trusted advisors is an elite member of a secret society that might be on a mission to destroy him and his company?" I said, frowning.

"You mean how do you tell him and not come across sounding like you need to be put in a padded cell?" Josie said, dipping the last crumpet in the remnants of jam and cream sauce.

"Yeah," I said.

"Good luck with that," she said. "I got it. Tell your mother and then ask her if she can work it into a little pillow talk."

"You're not helping," I said, laughing along.

178

"Disagree."

Fenella glanced back and forth at us with a confused look on her face.

"What is it, Fenella?" I said.

"Are you two always like this?" she said.

"Pretty much," Josie said, nodding.

"Some people might listen to your banter and wonder what was wrong with you," she said, smiling.

"Actually, Fenella," Josie said. "There are a lot of theories floating around about that question."

Chapter 21

The next day started early, ended late, and, in between, was filled with a seemingly endless list of tasks, moments of clarity, interruptions, and surprise visits that, by the time the day was finally over, made *Operation Whiteout* seem like a walk in the park.

We'd started at six with a sendoff breakfast for Mrs. Angus and Lancelot. At seven, we'd packed them into her rental car along with a picnic basket Chef Claire had prepared for both of them for the drive to the Ottawa airport and bid her a tearful goodbye along with a promise to visit her in Scotland the first chance we got.

At seven, Jackson entered my office with the results of his investigation into the phone numbers we'd copied from Jerry the Dognapper's phone. He informed us that the state police had put a trace on the number, but no calls had been made on the phone since they'd somehow managed to escape from Rooster's camp. Josie took the lead on that one, and she and Jackson headed to her office to try and make some sense of what appeared to be a random list of numbers.

At half past seven, I asked Sammy, our resident computer expert, to help me with a web search on the mysterious *Comann,* but after an hour of searching the only items we found were all speculative and dealt primarily with historical and, consistent with what Fenella had told us, mythological references.

"This isn't working," I said, glancing up from my screen.

"No, it certainly isn't," Sammy said. "But if these guys are actually operating a secret society, I'm sure they're hiding somewhere on the Dark Web."

"Dark Web?" I said. "What's that?"

"It's the part of the internet where the shadiest of the shady go to hide," Sammy said. "And it's no place you want to try to access."

"Is it that hard to get into?" I said, immediately intrigued by the idea.

"No, actually it's quite easy to do if you know what you're doing," he said. "You just need to download a specific browser and set up a VPN."

"You lost me, Sammy," I said, frowning at him.

"I know I did. And I did it on purpose because you don't know what you're doing and have no business even thinking about trying to access it," he said, giving me a hard stare. "A VPN is a Virtual Private Network that helps protect your identity while you're poking around down there. But you need to stay away from it, Suzy. I'm not joking."

"Because all the bad guys and boogie men are just waiting to get their hands on me?" I said, laughing.

"They'd be the least of your worries," Sammy said.

"Again, I'm not following you," I said.

"Suzy, if some of the biggest criminals in the world are hanging out there, who else do you think might be watching?" Sammy said.

"The cops?"

"Try every major law enforcement and intelligence agency on the planet," Sammy said. "I'm afraid you're going to have to look elsewhere for information about this secret society. Am I making myself clear, Suzy?"

"Sure, sure," I said, staring down at my keyboard.

"Suzy, I know how excited you get when you think you're about to solve a mystery, but this one is different," he said.

I looked up and recognized a side of him I didn't know he had. It was stern, fatherly, and protective. I found it both endearing and somewhat annoying.

"It can't hurt just to do a little poking around, can it?"

"I heard about a guy who was, as you put it, doing a little poking around, got on Homeland Security's radar, and is currently looking at twenty years for being a suspected terrorist."

"He must have been doing a lot more than just poking around," I said, dismissing the idea. "If I did want to access this Dark Web, and I'm not saying I do, how would I go about it?"

"No, absolutely not," Sammy snapped. "You'll get no help from me on this one. Just drop it."

"Okay, okay," I said, raising my hands in surrender.

"Thank you," he said. "Now, if you'll excuse me, I have some dogs to attend to that actually will listen to me from time to time."

"Funny," I said, waving him away.

I waited until he left the office, then began searching for instructions on how to access the Dark Web.

"He's such a drama queen sometimes," I said, laughing.

By ten-thirty, I had finally managed to follow the instructions I'd found and ended up in a place on the internet that was unfamiliar. I fought back against the creepy feeling that somebody was watching my every keystroke and entered Comann as a search term. I clicked a link and a website with the crescent-shaped logo in the top left-hand corner of the landing page appeared.

"That was easy," I said, glancing at my screen.

I scanned the landing page and found nothing there apart from the logo and some text I assumed was written in Gaelic. I copied *Bho aon, airson a h-uile* into one of the online translation tools and learned the phrase meant *From one, for all.*

"Kinda catchy, I guess," I said.

I stared at the landing page, then noticed a place to enter a password. I thought for a moment then typed Dinmont, Dandie Dinmont, and a host of other terms I thought might work. After a dozen tries, I gave up, noticed it was almost time for lunch, and turned my computer off.

I headed for the Water's Edge to meet my mother and Wentworth for lunch and during the drive I tried to figure out the best way to break the news to him about William, just call me Bill, Wild. I decided to just lay it out for him then do my best to answer any questions he had. As I expected, he was stunned by the news and, at first, had a hard time believing me. But when I outlined the secret society and referenced the tattoo of the Dandie on Bill's finger and told him that it was apparently reserved for the most elite members of Comann, he put his burger down and left the table to make a call to his office in New York.

"And you think I'm a piece of work," my mother said, shaking her head after Wentworth had left the table. "The things you manage to get involved with."

"What was I supposed to do, Mom?" I said. "Who knows how much damage Bill has already done to Wentworth and his company?"

"I knew there was something about him that bothered me," my mother said. "I can't believe you put all this together."

"We just got lucky," I said.

"Do you think it was Bill who killed the man under the ice?" she said, taking a bite of a French fry.

"I'm not sure," I said, then frowned at her. "How do you do that?"

"Do what?"

183

"Eat half a French fry."

"It's all about self-control, darling," she said, raising an eyebrow. "If there's one thing I've drilled into you over the years, it's that self-control is everything."

"Not when it comes to French fries," I said, laughing.

"Yes, so I've noticed, darling," she said, smiling as she ate the other half.

Fifteen minutes later, Wentworth returned to the table, disheveled and obviously rattled.

"Suzy, I don't how to thank you," he said, placing a hand on mine. "I called my head of security, and they just took Bill into custody. When he saw the three security guards heading toward his office, he panicked and took off running. They eventually cornered him in the stairwell on the twenty-first floor. I can't believe it."

"Do you have any idea what he might have been doing?" my mother said.

"Not yet," Wentworth said, pushing his plate aside. "But we will. What on earth is going on? Every day I have to deal with the Wall Street greedheads, computer hackers, terror threats, and now I've been infiltrated by some secret society from the 13th century."

"You poor dear," my mother said patting his hand. "But at least you were able to catch him, right?"

"Yeah," Wentworth said. "But I tell you, Snuggles, it's enough to make me want to sell the company and move to a small town and lead the quiet life."

"Well, don't do anything rash, sweetheart," my mother said, glancing at me.

I fought back a smile and grabbed a handful of fries.

"At least wait until things settle down a bit and you get a chance to cool off," she said.

"Yeah, I guess you're right," he said. "But this puts a damper on our ice fishing plans."

"I don't see why it would," my mother said.

"I should probably get back to New York," Wentworth said.

"Oh, I'm sure it will take your people some time to assess the damage, right?" my mother said as she ate another half of a single French fry.

"Yes, I imagine it will," he said, warily.

"And I'm also sure that you can get whatever updates you need via the phone or by video conference, sweetheart," my mother cooed.

"Yes, I'm sure I can, Snuggles," Wentworth whispered, beaten.

"Then that settles it," my mother said, getting up out of her chair. "I need to run to the little girl's room. Darling, if Millie drops off the check while I'm gone, just have her put it on my tab."

"Will do, Mom."

I watched her stroll off then looked at Wentworth.

"Nice try," I said, chuckling.

"Thanks. I thought it was worth a shot."

"You played it perfectly, but you were just beaten by a superior creature," I said, breaking into a laugh.

"She does have the knack for getting what she wants, doesn't she?"

"Yup. She certainly does."

"So how bad is it?"

"What? Ice fishing?

"Yeah," he said, taking a sip of coffee.

"Well, if we were going the traditional route, I'd say it's awful," I said. "But since we're going with my mom, it'll be like a day at the spa on ice."

"I don't understand," he said, frowning at me.

"It's one of those things you have to see to believe," I said, getting up out of my chair. "I need to run. I'll see you Saturday. And please tell my mom thanks for lunch."

"Will do," he said. "And thanks again for what you did."

"You're welcome," I said. "It's too bad. I liked the guy. A lot."

"Yeah, me too," he said. "But probably in a different way for different reasons."

"I'm sure of that," I said, waving goodbye as I walked away from the table.

By two, I was back in my office with Josie discussing what she and Jackson had identified during their review of Jack the Dognapper's phone records. It wasn't much, and our hopes that one of more of the phone numbers might provide a major clue to confirm our suspicions faded. I closed the manila folder and handed it back to her.

"Well, I guess it was worth a shot," I said.

"Yeah, but all we learned is that, over the past month, they ate a lot of pizza," she said, laughing.

"And all the incoming calls came from the same number?" I said.

"Yup. Jackson said it was a burner phone and impossible to trace," Josie said. "You know, pre-paid, and then tossed after the minutes are used up."

I nodded. I was familiar with the term from watching cop shows. It was good to know the lingo, but at the moment I'd settle for ignorance and a good clue.

"And there was only one call from Rooster several weeks ago, right?" I said.

Josie nodded as she opened a fresh bag of bite-sized Snickers. She offered me the bag, and I grabbed a handful. But since I have such small hands, I didn't think I was being too much of a glutton.

"I guess that's good news," I said, tearing open one of the tasty morsels and popping it in my mouth.

"Unless Rooster was the one with the burner phone," Josie said, rapidly building a small pile of wrappers in her lap.

"You don't think Rooster was involved with the dognapping, do you?"

"No, I don't," Josie said. "I think he was genuinely surprised when he saw his brother and cousin. But I do think he was somehow involved in helping them get away."

"Because of the old *blood is thicker than water* thing, right?" I said.

"Absolutely," she said, nodding.

"Sure, sure, I get that," I said. "Family."

"Jackson's still not convinced Rooster wasn't involved," Josie said. "Actually, to be more accurate, I'd say Jackson refuses to believe it."

"I think you're right," I said. "And there is a distinction there. Jackson's still annoyed that Rooster was the one who figured out the tracks coming and going from the Inn after the dognapping. Cops don't like to be shown up by other people, especially by someone like Rooster who tends to, let's say, work from the other side of the street."

"I think Jackson is being a bit of a baby about it," Josie said.

"Yeah, he's all over the map these days," I said. "And we both know why."

187

"Now he's mad that Freddie seems to have outmaneuvered him this winter," Josie said. "Jackson said that Chef Claire's love for all things winter caught him by surprise."

I shook my head as I got up to pour two cups of coffee. I handed Josie hers, then sat back down behind my desk.

"If they aren't careful, they're *both* going to blow their chance with her. For them, it's all about moves and countermoves. It's annoying, and I'm not even directly involved."

"I know. And I've tried to tell them," Josie said.

"You know what it means the longer this goes without a resolution, don't you?" I said, grabbing another small handful of the bite-sized.

"You mean if Chef Claire can't make up her mind after all this time?" Josie said

"Yeah."

"That while she loves Jackson and Freddie, she isn't *in love* with either of them?" Josie said.

"Bingo," I said, nodding. "And as we both know all too well, there's a *real* distinction between those two. Did Jackson have any other ideas regarding his plans for Chef Claire when you talked to him today?"

"You mean, apart from hiding Freddie's skis and praying for an early spring?" Josie deadpanned.

"Now that one was funny," I said, laughing.

"Thanks. Speaking of being in love," Josie said. "How are your mom and Wentworth doing?"

"She's doing her best to get off the pedestal Wentworth seems determined to put her on," I said. "But he seems pretty committed to her."

188

"How did Wentworth take the news at lunch about Bill the Snogger?" she said, smiling as she stared off into the distance.

"Bill the Snogger?"

"Good one, huh?" she said.

"No. Not funny," I said. "Wentworth was really mad. He was doing the British thing and doing his best to hide it, but he was not a happy guy."

"I'd be furious," Josie said.

We both looked at the door when we heard the knock.

"Come on in," I said.

Sammy entered carrying a large dog carrier. We couldn't get a good look at what was inside.

"Sorry to interrupt, guys," Sammy said, placing the carrier on the desk. "But you need to see this."

"What do you have there?" Josie said, opening the door and peeking inside. "What on earth?"

"I was at the reception desk and got a call that a piece of the puzzle had just been left outside the front door," Sammy said. "They're really cute."

Josie and I peered into the carrier at the adult Dandie staring up at us with melancholy eyes. Next to the dog were three gorgeous puppies. Josie rubbed the dog's head and then began to gently maneuver the mother and puppies' limbs and abdomens. Moments later, she finished her initial examination and nodded.

"Well, I'll be," she said. "Lancelot, you little devil."

"Only three in the litter?" I said, gently scratching the dog's ears.

"Well, there's only three here," Josie said. "And they all seem to be doing fine. Somebody's been keeping a close eye on them."

"That's a relief," Sammy said.

"Do you know who the caller was?" I said.

"No, the voice sounded disguised," he said. "You know, muffled."

"Let's get them in the back for a closer look," Josie said, closing the carrier door and moved aside to make room for Sammy. "You know the prep drill, right, Sammy?"

"Yeah, I got it," he said, heading out the door holding the carrier with both arms.

"We'll be right there," Josie said, then began pacing back and forth across the office. "What's going on here?"

"Beats me," I said, shrugging. "Do you think that's the missing female from that breeder we talked with?"

"That would be my first guess," Josie said.

"Somebody decides to steal a top rated male and female Dandie and then breed them?" I said, baffled.

"But why on earth would anybody go to all that trouble?" Josie said. "It couldn't be for the money."

"No, it's not the money. Dandie puppies aren't cheap, but even at two grand a dog, with an average litter of three to six puppies, you sure aren't going to get rich."

"No, you wouldn't. Maybe it's about the preservation of the breed," Josie said.

"I guess that's a possibility," I said. "But the Dandie breeders are incredibly dedicated to their dogs and seem to be doing everything possible to make sure the breed survives. And if I were interested in keeping the Dandie lineage going strong, I'd be working with the breeders, not stealing their top dogs."

"I don't get it," Josie said, sitting back down on the couch. "I hope you've got some ideas because I've got nothing to offer."

190

I shook my head and sat quietly before a light bulb exploded in my head.

"What did you just say?" I said, glancing at Josie.

"I said I didn't have anything to offer," she said, then her eyes grew wide. "An offering."

"Yes, as in a gift," I said. "If I were one of the heads of a secret society that reveres the Dandie and all its qualities, what better way would there be for an underling to curry favor with me?"

"That's a really weird idea, Suzy," Josie said. "And it's so weird that it kinda makes sense. The people that run that society have to be incredibly wealthy, so giving them money wouldn't have much of an impact."

"And they obviously already have a lot of power," I said.

"But giving them a top of the line Dandie puppy would probably separate someone from the pack of other wannabes," Josie said, nodding.

"As well as demonstrate a deep understanding of Comann and its historical underpinnings," I said.

"Historical underpinnings?" Josie said, frowning at me.

"I've been watching that series Chef Claire likes about the history of food," I said.

"I can't watch that show," Josie said. "It only makes me hungry."

"Eating makes you hungry," I said, laughing.

"Funny," she said, climbing to her feet. "Okay, I'm going to check out our new arrivals."

"I'll be there in a few minutes," I said. "I'm going to call that breeder and get the name of her missing female. I think she lives in Vermont, and I'm sure she's as anxious to find her dog as Mrs. Angus was."

"I wonder if they'll fight for custody of the puppies," Josie said, laughing.

"They might," I said. "I'm just glad that another dog didn't beat Lancelot to the punch."

"Now, there's an interesting thought," Josie said. "A Rottweiler-Dandie cross."

I laughed at the image of what one of those puppies might look like.

"Or maybe a Dalmatian-Dinmont," I said. "We could call it a Dalmont."

"Oooh, a Dandie with spots. How cute would that be?" Josie said, waving on her way out the door.

By six, Josie had given all four dogs two thumbs up, and they were resting comfortably in one of the condos. We'd also confirmed that the female was the breeder's missing dog and had made arrangements for her to arrive tomorrow morning. We washed up then returned to my office to take care of a bit of Inn business before heading up to the house for dinner.

Ten minutes later, we heard another knock on the door.

"Come in," I said without looking up from the document we were reviewing.

"Good evening, ladies."

We looked up and stared at the man standing in the doorway.

"Agent Tompkins?" I said to him, then glanced at Josie who also seemed extremely confused to see the FBI agent standing in the doorway.

"It's nice to see both of you again," he said as he strolled in and glanced around the office.

We'd met Agent Tompkins a few months ago when he helped us break up a puppy-smuggling operation that involved a complicated industrial espionage scheme. He had impressed both of us, and Chef Claire had fallen all over herself when she first met the handsome agent. But she'd quickly cooled off and was extremely disappointed when he'd informed us that he was engaged and soon to be married.

"Please, have a seat," I said. "So how are the wedding plans going?"

"Sadly, they aren't going anywhere," he said, frowning.

"Oh, no," Josie said. "What happened?"

"It's a long story," he said.

"All the good ones are," Josie said, smiling at him.

"Maybe another time," he said. "The wounds are still pretty fresh."

"Still bleeding?" Josie said.

"Only when I talk about it," he said.

"Okay, we get the point," I said. "Moving on. Since you're obviously not here to discuss your love life, how can we help you?"

"Actually, it's the other way around, Suzy," Agent Tompkins said, giving me a look that made me very uncomfortable. "I'm here to see if I can help you."

"I'm sorry, Agent Tompkins," I said. "But I'm not following you."

"Then let me make it easy for you," he said, forcing a fake smile. "Would you mind telling me why you were trying to access the Comann website earlier today?"

Stunned, I stared back at him and blinked several times.

"You were doing what?" Josie said, frowning at me.

"Don't worry about it," I said, waving Josie off. "It was nothing."

"Suzy, I'm afraid the FBI considers it a lot more than nothing."

"Okay," I said, trying to organize my thoughts. "But before I tell you, would you mind telling me how you know that?"

"Really?" Agent Tompkins said, raising an eyebrow. "You really want to know?"

"Actually, yes, I do."

"Suzy, if I wanted to, I could tell you how much money you've got in the bank down to the penny, who you've been talking to on the phone, and every single item you've bought at the grocery store in the past year."

"But you don't want to do that, right?"

"Not yet," he snapped. "For now, all I want to know is why you thought it would be a good idea to start snooping around that website."

"Okay, fair question," I said. "But that was only a couple of hours ago. How did you find out so fast?"

"We knew about it the second it happened," he said, glancing down at a piece of paper. "That would be at 10:57 this morning."

I swallowed hard.

"You're very lucky it landed on my desk," he said. "When the people in D.C. identified you, your name came up attached to mine on the puppy smuggling case. So they called me. If they hadn't, there would probably be a black helicopter sitting on your lawn at the moment. Now, do tell, what on earth were you doing?"

I did a quick bladder check, then exhaled loudly and told him everything in detail starting with the discovery of the body under the ice and finishing with the arrival of the Dandie puppies. I sat back in my chair and waited for his response. He sat quietly for a very long time. Finally, I couldn't stand the silence any longer.

"Uh, Agent Tompkins?" I said.

"What?"

"I couldn't help but notice that you didn't take any notes the entire time I was talking," I said.

"So?"

"So how are you going to remember everything I told you?" I said.

"Suzy, please don't start," Josie said.

"Don't worry," he said. "I got every word."

"You recorded it?" I said.

"Of course I recorded it," he said, staring at me.

"You can't just do that without permission," I said.

"Why not? Whose permission do I need?" he said.

"Well, mine for starters," I said.

Josie snorted.

"I see," Agent Tompkins said. "I guess there is another option. Would you like to hear it?"

"I would love to," I snapped.

"I can take my recording device and leave to make a phone call. The helicopter should be here in about twenty minutes."

"There's no need to get snarky, Agent Tompkins," I said.

"You need to dial it down a notch, Suzy," he said, fixing a cold stare on me that sent a chill through me.

"Can you teach me that look, Agent Tompkins?" Josie said, laughing. "I could definitely use that one."

"You're not helping," I said, glaring at her.

"Disagree," she said, nodding her head at the FBI agent. "You see. He's cracking a smile."

"You two," Agent Tompkins said, shaking his head. "What a pair."

"Do you believe me when I say I was merely being nosy?" I said.

"I do," he said. "Unfortunately, that's not much of an excuse these days. You need to stay off the Dark Web, Suzy. And I can't stress this enough, you need to stay away from all things Comann. Do you understand what I'm saying?"

"Hey, I'm not that much of a slow learner," I said. "I got it."

"Good. Consider yourself warned. But you're only going to get this one."

I nodded and began fiddling with a pen. I started tapping in on the desk, then stopped when a thought popped into my head.

"Can I ask you if anything I just told you was new information?"

Agent Tompkins thought about my question for several moments before nodding.

"Yeah, quite a bit actually. We didn't know that Wentworth's company had been infiltrated."

"You know Wentworth?" I said, frowning.

"Yeah, he's helped us out a couple times in the past," Agent Tompkins said. "He's a good guy."

"He's dating my mother," I said.

"Really? He's a brave man," he said, laughing.

"How do you know my mother?" I said, completely surprised by that news.

"I don't," he said. "Not personally anyway."

"But you could if you wanted to, right?" I said.

"Sure. But there's no need for that. From what I've seen and heard, your mother seems to be pretty much of a straight shooter."

"You're freaking me out a bit here, Agent Tompkins," I said.

"Good. Mission accomplished," he said. "And I have to thank you for clarifying the dog angle. We knew there were some historical underpinnings with the Dandie breed, but the details were fuzzy."

Josie groaned.

"Historical underpinnings?" I said. "The History of Food, right?"

"Yeah, I love that show," Agent Tompkins said, leaning forward in his chair.

"Me too," I said. "Chef Claire and I watch it all the time."

"The history of bread episode was fantastic. How is Chef Claire doing?" he said.

"She's great," I said. "I know she'd love to see you. In fact, why don't you stay for dinner?"

"I don't know. I should probably head back," he said, glancing at his watch. "I can just grab something along the way."

"Hey, you gotta eat, Agent Tompkins," I said. "French onion soup. Beef tenderloin with a horseradish and rosemary stuffing. And you won't believe the magic she works with potatoes and a Gruyere sauce. I'm telling you, it's a total knee-buckler. What do you say, Josie?"

"I could eat."

"Now there's a surprise," I said, shaking my head. "I was referring to the idea of Agent Tompkins joining us for dinner."

"Oh. Well, I think it's a great idea. As long as Chef Claire doesn't lose her focus," Josie said, laughing.

"Then it's settled," I said, getting up from my chair. "And you can make sure you get all your questions answered, Agent Tompkins."

"That would be good," he said. "Because the other option would be to ask you come to our office on Saturday morning. We've got some heavyweights coming in from D.C. to discuss Comann, and I'm sure they will definitely be interested in what's been going on around here."

"I'm sorry Agent Tompkins. But we'll have to get everything wrapped up tonight," I said. "I can't make it on Saturday."

"Why not?"

"Because I'm going ice fishing," I said.

"And you think that going ice fishing should take precedence over a meeting with the FBI?" he said, his eyes narrowing.

"No, not by itself I don't," I said. "But I'm going with my mother, and if I don't show up, she'll kill me."

Chapter 22

For those unfamiliar with the seemingly insane prospect of standing on a frozen body of water in the frigid cold and wind while hovering over a hole in the ice waiting for a fish to bite, ice fishing is a straightforward proposition. You cut a hole in the ice, bait your hook, drop it into the water, and wait for an unsuspecting fish that must be freezing its fins off to swim by. And while historical black and white photos often show frostbitten people hunkered down holding a fishing pole over a solitary hole in the ice, thereby romanticizing a quaint, outdated practice from a time long gone, ice fishing, like most other recreational activities, has gone high-tech.

And when it comes to the acquisition of high-tech toys and equipment destined for occasional use and as a dust-collector in one's garage or backyard, nobody comes close to my mother's prowess. Given my mother's lifestyle and her ongoing carping about my *unladylike behaviors*, ice fishing would seem to be an activity she would participate in only under threat of gunpoint. But my father had convinced her to give it a shot early in their marriage, and she'd eventually come to enjoy it. The memories had stayed with her, and she continued the tradition to this day.

One evening over dinner, she'd even hinted, although refused to confirm, that my existence was the direct result of a brandy-fueled liaison in a makeshift ice fishing shanty on a frigid day when the fish weren't biting and the north wind had driven them inside. I made it a point of not thinking about her and my father getting busy on a sheet of ice between sips from a bottle of brandy, but I've always thought it might explain my tolerance for cold weather.

And if the facts surrounding my conception were true, the least I could do was agree to go ice fishing with her once a year.

I glanced through my side mirror at the object I was towing behind my SUV. At the moment, it was simply an aluminum and fiberglass box that had been folded up and put on skis. But when assembled, it would be transformed into an 18 x 24 structure that was the envy of every ice fisherman within fifty miles and borrowed on a regular basis.

I glanced through the rearview mirror and smiled when I caught the bewildered expression on Wentworth's face as we continued further out on the ice toward the middle of the bay.

"How are you doing back there?" I said.

"Oh, I'm fine," he said. "How often does your mother do this?"

"Every chance she gets," I said, shrugging. "It's hard to explain, but it's just one of those weird things about her that make her unique."

"I guess unique is a word for it," Wentworth said, flatly.

Josie and I laughed. She offered me the bag of bite-sized Snickers, and I took two. Wentworth declined with a shake of his head and resumed staring out at the Arctic landscape.

"At least we got lucky with the weather," I said, again glancing at him through the mirror. "It's supposed to hit fifteen this afternoon."

"Downright balmy," Wentworth said.

Josie and I laughed again.

"Don't worry, Wentworth," Josie said. "Once we get *The Thing* set up, you and I can play Scrabble while the rest of them fish. If you can call it fishing."

"What else would you call it?" he said, frowning.

"An unfair sporting practice," Josie said, shaking her head.

"Don't start," I said.

"I don't understand," Wentworth said.

"You'll see," Josie said, turning around in her seat. "Here comes the floor show."

We heard the roar of the snowmobile, and I slowed down as it got closer. The snowmobile also slowed and my mother, driving, pointed at a spot on the ice about two hundred yards in front of us. Her new snowmobile, while not as powerful as the one she'd sold Rooster, still had more horsepower than she needed. Chef Claire had her arms wrapped around my mother's waist, and she beamed and waved as they raced past us. I pulled to a stop at the spot my mother was pointing at, turned the car off, and climbed out.

The cold wind whipped, and my eyes stung and watered. Mother Nature seemed to be reminding me that, while I could hide in a warm car all I wanted, as soon as I stepped outside, I belonged to her. For some reason, that thought reminded me of my mother, and I smiled as I studied her. The snowmobile was a bright lime green, and my mother wore a matching snowsuit and helmet. She scanned the immediate area as she paced back and forth like Patton surveying his troops, that is if Patton was five-foot tall and dressed as a lime.

"Nice job, darling," my mother said.

Apparently, she was referring to the fact that I'd navigated a mile and a half towing what Josie had nicknamed The Thing without getting into an accident or managing to fall through the ice that was still about a foot thick.

"No problem, Mom," I said. "Where do you want to start?"

"Let's see," she said, glancing back and forth, then spotted Wentworth reluctantly climbing out of the SUV. "There's my guy. You missed a fun ride, sweetheart."

"Oh, well," he said, forcing a smile. "Maybe next time."

"Don't worry," my mother said, beaming at him. "You won't have to wait long."

"That was so much fun," Chef Claire said as she approached. "I don't know why they give you such a hard time, Mrs. C. I think you're a great driver."

"Why thank you, dear," my mother said, hanging her helmet on one of the handlebars.

"Suck up," Josie said. "Okay, I'm officially freezing. What do you need me to do, Mrs. C.?"

"I thought you and Suzy could show Wentworth how to assemble the shanty," my mother said. "After all, it's something that you'll need to be able to do in the future, sweetheart."

"Sure, sure," Wentworth said, hugging himself for warmth. "I can't wait."

Then we heard a loud crack that sounded like a gunshot. It continued to reverberate for several seconds before it eventually faded away.

"What on earth was that?" Wentworth said, paralyzed with fear and frozen in his tracks.

"Relax, sweetheart," my mother said, waving her hand. "It's just the ice settling."

"Settling where?" he said, wild-eyed. "On the bottom of the River?"

My mother laughed and again waved the idea away.

"It's okay, Wentworth," I said. "There's nothing to worry about. But you're not alone. The first time everybody hears that sound, it freaks them out. Watch."

I started jumping up and down on the ice and Wentworth's eyes grew even wider. A small burst of cracking sounds followed then faded away.

"Please don't do that," he whispered, staring at me with pleading eyes.

"Okay, here's the plan," my mother said, getting down to business. "While you set up the shanty, Chef Claire and I will get all the tip-ups in place."

She put her hands on her hips as she again surveyed the immediate area, then scuffed a patch of accumulated snow with her boot. "Get the shanty up right here. Make sure the window is facing directly toward where my snowmobile is parked. And don't forget to drive the spikes into each corner. We wouldn't want it blowing away in this wind, would we?"

"No, we certainly don't, Mrs. C.," Josie said, heading for the SUV. "C'mon Wentworth. Now you be careful and watch where you're going."

"You don't have to worry about that," he said.

Wentworth tiptoed his way back to the vehicle and Josie watched his tentative steps then turned back to us and shook her head.

"You sure this is a good idea, Mrs. C.?" Josie said.

"I'm positive, my dear," my mother said, smiling as she watched Wentworth approach the back hatch of the SUV. "It looks like he's trying to sneak up on the car. What a baby."

"Give him a break, Mom," I said. "This is the first time he's done this."

"It's not brain surgery, darling," she said. "Okay, Chef Claire. Do you think you can handle the power auger?"

"That thing?" Chef Claire said, nodding at the object attached the one side of the snowmobile. "Sure, I can handle that. It's just a very big immersion blender. Does that mean I get to dig the holes in the ice?"

"It does," my mother said. "One hole for each tip-up."

"So I guess we'll need, what, three or four?" Chef Claire said.

"Try five," my mother said.

"Five. Sure, no problem," Chef Claire said.

"Five per person," my mother said, smiling. "Each person is allowed to have five tip-ups."

"Twenty-five?" Chef Claire said, suddenly less eager. "That's a lot of holes."

"Actually, we'll need a couple more for hand fishing inside the shanty," my mother said.

"Really?" Chef Claire said. "Hand fishing inside a warm shanty? What about battling the elements? You know, woman versus fish."

"Trust me," I said. "By the end of the day, those two holes will be your favorites."

Josie returned dragging a small box that was mounted on a pair of short skis.

"I thought you might need these," she said, handing the rope to my mother.

My mother tied the rope to the back of her snowmobile and removed one of the tip-ups from the box.

"How do they work?" Chef Claire said.

My mother flipped a piece of wood on the tip-up, and it unfolded into an X. Then she flipped another piece of wood upright.

"That's it," my mother said as she continued her demonstration. "You put one of the live minnows on the hook, place the tip-up across one of the holes you've cut in the ice, and then bend the piece of metal on top until it's secured in this small latch right here. When a fish hits, it releases the piece of metal, and the little red flag flapping in the breeze is what tells you you've got a bite."

"Okay," Chef Claire said. "I think I got it. You want me to start digging some holes around here?"

"Oh, my no," my mother said. "We're going to put them out there."

My mother raised her arm and moved it back and forth off into the distance.

"I'm thinking about three hundred yards out in a semi-circle that we'll be able to see from the window."

"So we don't actually stand out here close to the tip-ups?" Chef Claire said, frowning.

"Of course not," my mother said. "We're not a herd of barbarians."

"Okay. And you're sure we'll be able to see a flag when it goes up?" Chef Claire said.

"That's what the binoculars are for, Chef Claire," my mother said, laughing. "We take turns scanning the horizon from the comfort and warmth of the shanty, and when we see a raised flag, we hop on the snowmobile and go catch the fish."

Chef Claire frowned.

"Is all this legal?" she said.

My mother and I laughed.

"Yes, Chef Claire," my mother said. "And not only is it legal, it's downright *civilized*. Okay, let's see how your auger skills are, Chef Claire."

My mother grabbed the auger and handed it to Chef Claire.

"It starts like a lawnmower. You just pull that handle," my mother said, walking inside the spot where the shanty was going up. "Let's see. We'll need a hole here, and another about ten feet straight back from the first."

"You want me to cut the holes now?" Chef Claire said.

"Well, we're certainly not going to cut them while we're all inside the shanty," my mother snapped. "Let's go. We're wasting time here."

"Welcome to the family," I whispered to Chef Claire.

Chef Claire fired up the auger and cut the first hole. When she broke through the ice, a surge of ice chips and water surged up out of the hole and covered her boots. She nodded and smiled at my mother. Chef Claire cut the second hole, stamped ice and water off her boots, and turned the auger off.

"Now I get it," Chef Claire said. "Good thinking, Mrs. C."

"It's a mistake you don't make twice," my mother said, striding toward her snowmobile. "Okay, hop on. We've got work to do. Make sure you get the shanty up and the food on the stove, darling."

"Yes, Mom," I said.

Then my mother fired up the snowmobile and slowly headed out towing the box of tip-ups and bait bucket with Chef Claire sitting behind her holding the power auger across her lap. I helped Josie position the still folded shanty where my mother wanted it. Then I pounded a large metal spike into each corner of the structure. I stood back and looked at Wentworth.

"You want to do the honors?" I said.

"I beg your pardon," he said, still frazzled about being out here.

"Just pull that lever," I said, pointing.

Wentworth did as instructed, and the structure seemed to magically come to life.

"Wow," Wentworth said. "Most impressive."

"My mother had it built," I said.

"By whom?" he said.

"Oh, just a local engineer who's a friend of hers," I said, glancing at Josie.

Josie smiled but said nothing.

The shanty was all that remained from that previous relationship.

I slid the door open, and we stepped inside the spacious shanty. Josie and I, veterans of the process, carefully made our way around the two ice holes and released various handles and several sitting areas appeared. We removed the cushions from an inbuilt drawer and set them in place, then assembled a table that was fastened to one side of the structure. We set two large pots on the portable stove and lit the propane-fueled fire. Immediately, it started to warm up inside the shanty. Then we stood back to admire our work.

"Good job," I said, glancing around.

"Is that it?" Wentworth said.

"All that's left is to get the hot tub set up," Josie said.

"What?" he said, thoroughly confused.

"I'm joking, Wentworth," Josie said, laughing.

"Oh," he said, glancing back and forth at us with a mischievous grin. "Too bad." Then he caught the look we were giving him. "Sorry. That was inappropriate."

"Forget it," I said. "But whatever you do, don't do that around my mother."

207

"Of course not," he stammered. "Again, I apologize."

"Relax, Wentworth," Josie said. "We've seen much worse. Let's see how you do at hand fishing."

"Really?" he said. "Can't I just watch?"

"You can," I said. "But the people who aren't hand fishing inside are assigned snowmobile duty."

"You mean I'd being going out there on the back of that infernal machine closer to the thin ice?" he said.

"Yeah, unless you want to drive," I said.

"Not bloody likely," he said.

"And then you'll need to remove your gloves when you try and land the fish."

"Well, then let's give this hand fishing thing a shot, shall we?" he said, accepting the fishing line I was holding in my hand. "The minnow goes on the hook, right?"

Fifteen minutes later, my mother and Chef Claire returned. Chef Claire looked like a kid at Christmas.

"This is so cool. I love it," she said, then fanned herself. "It's a bit warm in here, isn't it?"

"She's definitely in need of professional help," Josie said.

I nodded and watched my mother head for a thermos that contained hot Kahlua coffee. She poured a cup and took a sip as she watched Wentworth sitting in a folding chair directly over one of the holes in the ice.

"I think we have a pro in the making," my mother said. "Are you catching anything, sweetheart?"

"Not yet, Snuggles," he said, glancing up at her. Then he whispered, "Apart from pneumonia."

Josie and I stifled a laugh. Chef Claire picked up the binoculars, draped them around her neck, and began scanning the horizon for signs of a raised flag. Moments later, she shrieked and grabbed my mother's arm.

"Do you see a raised flag, my dear?" my mother said, setting her cup down.

"I see three," Chef Claire almost shouted.

"Wonderful," my mother said. "Let's go. The way we handle multiple flags is for me to drop you off at the first one, then I'll drive to the furthest one away. Then we'll meet back at the one in the middle."

"Got it," Chef Claire, dashing for the door with my mother in hot pursuit.

We heard the roar of the snowmobile, and I stared after them until they became a distant speck.

"While they're gone, I think I might partake of a cup of that Kahlua coffee," Wentworth said, rising to his feet. "Can I pour you ladies one?"

"No, I'm good, thanks," I said, sitting down.

"I'm going to wait," Josie said, accepting the fishing line from Wentworth. "Hey, watch your step, Wentworth!"

"Ah, no!" Wentworth exclaimed when he stepped in one of the holes and his leg ended up buried to the thigh in the frigid water under the ice. "My word, that's cold."

We helped him pull his leg out of the water and led him to one of the sitting areas.

"We need to get that boot off," I said, beginning to untie his shoelace.

"No, that's quite all right," he said, trying to fend me off. "I'll be fine."

"Trust me, Wentworth," I said. "You won't be fine. This could get serious in a hurry."

"Listen to her, Wentworth," Josie said, sliding across the ice to help me.

"No, really," he said. "I insist. I'll be fine."

Josie and I ignored his protests and continued to untie his boot. We managed to get it off despite his attempts to get away. The boot was full of water, and his thick socks were soaked.

"Relax, Wentworth," I said.

"Yeah, you'd think we were trying to check you for a hernia," Josie said, holding his leg down. "Don't be such a baby."

"No, stop!" he snapped.

Undeterred, I removed his sock, then stopped, stunned by what I was looking at. I glanced at Josie, who continued to stare at the magnificent tattoo of the Dandie Dinmont that covered most of the top of his right foot.

"Oh, no," I whispered.

"I guess that changes a few things, doesn't it?" Josie said.

We both looked up at Wentworth who was pointing a gun at us and shaking his head.

"You just couldn't let it go, could you?" he said softly.

"Let what go?" I said, keeping a very close eye on the gun.

"All of it," he said. "You find a guy under the ice and just have to snoop around. Somebody steals a dog, and you make it your life's mission to figure out what happened."

"Well, in all fairness, Wentworth," Josie said. "We take dognapping very seriously."

"Shut up, Josie," Wentworth said, glaring at her. "You think you're so funny with all your jokes."

"Trust me, Wentworth," Josie said, returning his glare. "I wasn't joking."

"What a mess," he said, working his foot back into the wet boot, then getting to his feet. "If you ladies will excuse me, I need to get out of here. Suzy, your car keys if you don't mind."

"You're part of Comann?" I said, slowly reaching for a zipper on my parka.

"I run Comann," he said, gesturing with the gun for me to hurry up. "At least for now I do. If this situation blows up and goes public, I'm sure I'll become a historical footnote."

"I don't understand. What is Comann doing around here?" I said, frowning.

"Comann isn't doing anything around here. I was only hanging around because of your mother," he said, again gesturing with the gun. "Hurry up."

"The way you're pointing that gun is making me nervous," I said. "Now my zipper's stuck."

"Suzy," he said, sliding the door open and extending his arm holding the gun toward me. "Don't mess with me."

"No, really," I said. "The zipper's stuck. See?"

Wentworth exhaled loudly but kept pointing the gun at my head.

"Come on," he said as a gust of wind whipped through the shanty.

"I'm trying," I said, sneaking a glance out the window. "So how does Bill fit into all this?"

"Bill?" he said, frowning. "Bill who?"

"Bill Wild. Who else would I be talking about?" I said, hoping to appear frantic as I struggled with the zipper.

"Oh, that Bill," he said, shrugging. "Just another foot soldier who forgot his place."

"Foot soldier?" Josie said. "I thought the finger tattoo was reserved for the elite members of your society."

"It is," Wentworth said, shaking his head. "The idiot awarded it to himself. But people like that are always doing things to attract attention."

"And that's a bad move to make in Comann, right?" Josie said.

"The worst," he said. "Some people never seem capable of understanding that."

"Some people?" I said. "There's more than just Bill?"

"Sure," he said. "Every organization gets them from time to time. Come on, Suzy. Move along. You're about thirty seconds from getting shot in the head."

I snuck another look out the window and noticed it was starting to snow.

"So what happened to him?" I said.

"Just like I told you. He ran when the security guards showed up, then he was cornered in the stairwell."

"And?" I said.

"What do you think happened?" Wentworth said. "I can't have loose cannons like that running around. No matter how fond I am of them."

"But you've done work for the FBI," I said.

"Yes, I have," he said, giving me an evil grin and leaning against the side of the shanty. "Trust is such a tricky concept." Then he frowned. "How did you know I've done work for the FBI?"

"Does it matter?" I said, finally opening the zipper.

"Not much. And in a few minutes it won't matter at all," he said. "Now, please. The keys."

"What are you going to do with my mother?" I said.

"Unfortunately, the same thing I'm about to do to you two," he said, then turned almost melancholy. "It's such a pity. I thought she might be the one. With her money and connections, we could have done some amazing things together. But I've learned something about your mother that made that impossible."

"That she's incorruptible?" I said.

"Exactly," he said, nodding. "I see why the two of you are so close."

"We have our moments," I said, tossing him my car keys.

"Thank you," he said, snatching the keys out of mid-air with his free hand. "I really wish this could have turned out differently."

He raised the gun and pointed it at me as the wind continued to whip his hair. For some strange reason, I had a childhood memory of cotton candy as I watched it blow in the wind. Wentworth exhaled, stared intensely at me, and then dropped like a rock onto the ice floor of the shanty. The gun fell from his hand, slid across the ice, and disappeared down one of the ice holes. Josie and I slid across the ice, pulled Wentworth's hands back behind his back, and tied them tight with his shoelace.

"Wow," Josie said, staring down at the ice ball lying next to Wentworth's unconscious body. "Chef Claire?"

"Who else?" I said, waiting for my breathing to return to normal.

"How far away was she?" Josie said.

"Thirty, maybe forty feet," I said as Chef Claire entered the shanty.

"I saw the gun through the binoculars," she said, shaking with nervous energy. "Sorry, it took me a while to get here. I couldn't get your Mom's attention, so I had to hoof it back. What on earth is going on?"

213

"Let's wait for my Mom," I said. "I'm sure I'm not going to want to tell this story twice."

"Great shot by the way," Josie said.

"Thanks," she said. "It was your basic throw from third to first."

We heard the roar of the approaching snowmobile, then silence. Seconds later, my mother stepped inside the shanty holding a large Northern Pike in each hand. Then she stared down at Wentworth who had a large bump on the back of his head and was slowly coming to. Then looked at me waiting for an explanation.

"I'm sorry, Mom," I said.

"Don't be, darling," my mother said, glancing back down at Wentworth. "He's part of that secret society, isn't he?"

"How on earth did you know that?" I said.

"I've had my suspicions for a while," she said. "But when he started hinting that he wanted me to introduce him to a certain Senator that confirmed it for me."

"A *certain* Senator?" Josie said.

"Yeah, that's the one," my mother said, grinning. "He's an old friend."

"Are you going to be okay?" I said.

"Of course, darling. I'm just glad you're all right," my mother said. "This actually makes my job of ending this relationship much easier. And it's just not a good idea to spend too much time around *those people*."

Chapter 23

While we waited for Jackson to arrive, we rolled Wentworth over and worked him into a sitting position on the ice with his back against one of the shanty walls. He was still groggy, but able to converse. So we started peppering him with questions. Either he wasn't concerned about potentially divulging incriminating information that might be used against him, or his concussion had eliminated his ability to think straight. Whatever the reason, he opened up to us, although his answers were often punctuated with grunts and groans.

"So, the only reason you're here is because of my Mom?" I said.

"Yes," Wentworth said, wincing as he nodded his head. Then he glanced up at my mother. "I was falling in love with you, Snuggles."

"Perhaps," my mother said. "But you were also trying to use me. And that's inexcusable."

"I was hoping we'd be able to form a partnership that would benefit both of us," he said. "And I'm sorry about never taking my socks off in bed. I know that drove you crazy. But now you understand why, right?"

"I guess," she said. "But it's just not a good look, Wentworth."

Josie and I laughed, and I caught my mom's eye. She winked at me then turned to Chef Claire.

"Thank you."

"Don't mention it, Mrs. C.," Chef Claire said. "That's a couple of nice fish you've got there."

"Thanks for reminding me," my mother said, glancing down at the two pike she'd dropped.

She used her boot to gently shove the flopping fish toward the nearest ice hole. The fish disappeared under the ice, and my mother bent down to make sure both fish had survived their ordeal.

"They both made it," my mother said, climbing to her feet.

"You go through all of this nonsense," Wentworth said. "And then you let them go?"

"Sure. It's called catch and release," my mother said.

"Why on earth would you do something as patently ridiculous as that?" he said, baffled.

"Tradition," my mother said, shrugging. "And Suzy doesn't eat fish."

"I gotta tell you, Mrs. C.," Chef Claire said. "It doesn't make a lot of sense to me either."

"Over time it will, dear," my mother said. "But you should feel free to keep any of the fish you catch. The three of us are just happy to be out here enjoying the overall experience."

"Gee, Mrs. C.," Josie said. "Enjoy is such a strong word."

"You'll feel better after lunch, dear," my mother said, patting Josie's arm.

"Wentworth, I need to ask you something," I said.

"Go ahead," he said, trying to reposition himself on the ice. "But before you do, can I get a pillow or a towel to sit on? My lower back feels like someone has driven a spike through it."

"You should be so lucky," my mother said.

Deciding that I had a better chance of him answering my questions if I agreed, I grabbed a pillow off one of the sitting areas and helped him position it underneath him. He settled back down on the ice and nodded at me.

"If Comann wasn't working on anything up here, why was Bill spending so much time around this place in the middle of winter?"

"I was trying to keep a close eye on him," Wentworth said. "He'd been acting quite strange the past few months, and I wanted to find out why. I was very fond of him."

"So you just told him to come up here, and he didn't get suspicious?" I said.

"My people do what I ask them to do without question," Wentworth said. "But the real reason he was so happy to stick around was because of you."

"What?" I said, glaring at my mother. "Mom, please tell me you didn't use me as bait for this guy."

"Of course not, darling," my mother snapped. "I was merely trying to set you up with someone I thought you'd like."

"Thanks for that, Mom. Once again, here comes Mom riding in on her white horse to save her daughter from all those long, lonely nights."

"I know you're alone, Suzy, but since when are you lonely?" Josie said.

"I'm not," I said, my voice rising. "I'm merely making a point."

"I was right, wasn't I?" my mother shouted. "You liked him a lot."

"That's not the point, Mom," I snapped.

"Hey, guys," Josie said. "Before things escalate any further, how about we get back on topic and call this one a draw?"

My mother and I continued to glare at each other, but eventually we softened and called a silent truce. I refocused on Wentworth.

"How did Bill happen to start working for you?" I said.

"Well, I'm not really sure," Wentworth said. "I know he started with my financial firm a few years ago as a junior analyst before he got promoted."

"He didn't start working for you while he was in London?" I said.

"London?" Wentworth said, frowning. "Absolutely not."

"Another lie," I said, shaking my head.

"Suzy, try not to hold that against him," Wentworth said. "He's been trained to lie his whole life. At least since Comann found him."

"Found him where?" I said.

Wentworth stared down at the ice.

"It wouldn't happen to be from one of the orphanages you operate, would it?"

"What? Who have you been talking to?" Wentworth said.

"Nobody," I said.

Stunned, Wentworth stared at me.

I'd been thinking that there might be more than the one orphanage in Scotland that Mrs. Angus had mentioned and I'd decided to go with a major bluff.

"So which orphanage was it?"

"I think it was the one that's out in Oregon," he said.

"That's too bad," Josie whispered.

"Yeah," I whispered back. "I was hoping for a connection to the one in Scotland."

"It was a good try," Josie whispered.

"Thanks."

"Ladies, it's not polite to whisper with other people in the room," my mother said.

"Sorry, Mom." I looked at Wentworth. "Are you telling the truth when you say you were very close to Bill?"

"Yes," he said. "I didn't even know him at first, but after he got a major promotion last year, he and I worked very closely together on different projects."

"A major promotion?" I said.

"Yes. He got a very big job," Wentworth said.

"Inside your financial company or in Comann?" I said.

"Why both, of course," Wentworth said. "It was an unusually big jump in responsibilities, but he came highly recommended."

"By who?"

"Does it matter?" Wentworth said.

"Probably not," I said. "Do you think Bill was the one who killed the guy we found under the ice?"

"No. Bill wouldn't have been physically capable of doing that," Wentworth said.

"So he's not a killer," I said, glancing around. "I guess that's something, right?"

"Oh, he's a killer," Wentworth said. "I'm just saying he didn't kill the guy under the ice."

"Because it happened before Bill arrived in town, right?" I said, nodding.

Wentworth shrugged, then winced again.

"So where is he now?" I said.

"Does that really matter, Suzy?" Josie said.

"I'm just trying to close the loop," I said, my voice rising a notch. "That's all I'm doing."

Josie gave me a sad smile, then patted my arm.

"Go ahead. Close the loop," she said, glancing at my mother.

"So where is Bill?" I asked Wentworth again.

"I have no idea," he said. "After three of my security guards cornered him in the stairwell, he still somehow managed to get away."

"You sound almost proud of him," I said.

"Yeah, I guess I am a bit," Wentworth said. "My security guards, not so much. But that's my fault. If you pay peanuts, you get a monkey."

"Are you looking for him?" I said.

"Sure," he said, shrugging. "But he's long gone. At some point, it's possible that someone from Comann might track him down. But my guess is that Bill has already changed his appearance, and has a new identity."

Wentworth noticed our looks of concern.

"Don't worry," he said. "There's no reason for him to come back here." Then he paused to catch my eye. "There's not, is there, Suzy?"

"No," I said, shaking my head. "There's not."

We all looked up when Jackson and Detective Abrams from the state police appeared in the doorway. They stepped inside, closed the door behind them and surveyed the scene.

"Looks like you caught a big one," Jackson said, grinning as he glanced around. When he didn't get any reaction, he shrugged and looked at Detective Abrams. "Tough crowd."

"Wow," Chef Claire said, lowering the binoculars. "We've got another four flags up. Are you ready, Mrs. C.?"

"No, dear," my mother said. "I think I'll pass."

"Okay," Chef Claire said. "How about you, Josie?"

"Uh, I was just getting ready to watch a little TV," Josie said.

"This thing has got TV?" Jackson said, glancing around the shanty.

"Yeah," Josie said, shaking her head. "It's right over there near the hot tub."

"Funny," Jackson said, glaring at Josie.

"I liked it," I said, laughing.

"Thanks."

Chef Claire raced outside, and we soon heard the roar of the snowmobile.

"I hope she catches something," Josie said. "I'm in the mood for a good fish chowder."

"Yuk," I said, heading for the stove to stir the pot of chili.

"Jackson, if you gentlemen would be so kind to remove this horrible human being from my presence I'd be eternally grateful," my mother said.

"Horrible?" Wentworth said, looking up at my mother with a sad frown. "How can you say that, Snuggles?"

"It was easy," my mother said, giving him a shove with her boot. "And stop calling me Snuggles."

"Snuggles?" Jackson said, grinning. "Now that is good."

"Jackson, if you ever mention it to anyone, I swear you'll be counting change from the parking meters the rest of your career."

"Sorry, Mrs. C.," he said. "Okay, Detective Abrams. Let's say we go find a nice warm jail cell for this guy."

"My lawyers are going to have a field day with this," Wentworth said, scoffing and shaking his head at Jackson.

Detective Abrams paused from the admiring looks he was giving the shanty and nodded at Jackson.

"Yeah, sure. I'm ready," he said, then turned to my mother. "This is quite the set-up, Mrs. C. Any chance I can rent it from you? I've got some family coming in next week."

"No, Detective Abrams," my mother said. "But you can borrow it anytime you like."

He smiled at my mother and then he and Jackson each grabbed one of Wentworth's shoulders and lifted him to his feet.

"Ow," Wentworth said, limping. "I think I might be developing frostbite."

"Next time, watch where you're going," Josie said. "You never know what hole you might fall into. Or have to crawl out of."

"You know, Josie," Wentworth snapped. "You really aren't that funny."

"Disagree."

We watched as they led Wentworth into the back of the police car, then focused on lunch. We were halfway through our first bowl of chili when Chef Claire returned carrying two large fish.

"Look at the size of these," she said, her eyes wild with excitement.

"Well done," Josie said. "More than enough to make a huge pot of chowder."

"No, I don't think so," Chef Claire said. "It doesn't seem right to keep them today."

She walked toward one of the ice holes and gently slid both fish into the water. Then she glanced back and forth at us.

"If you guys ever tell one of my chef friends that I did that, you'll be eating peanut butter and jelly sandwiches," Chef Claire said.

"Well done, dear," my mother said, handing Chef Claire a bowl of chili.

We resumed eating and then we heard the unmistakable roar approaching. I got up and stepped outside and watched Rooster bring the powerful machine to a stop. He removed his helmet and grinned at me.

"I heard you had some excitement going on out here," he said, glancing around. "It looks like I'm too late."

"But just in time for lunch," I said.

"Nah, thanks," he said. "I just wanted to make sure you guys were okay."

"We're fine," I said, raising an eyebrow at him. "How did you know?"

"I have my sources," he said. "Now do you finally believe me about why you need to stay away from those people?"

"Yeah, I do," I said. "I guess I'm a bit of a slow learner."

"No, not at all," Rooster said, grinning. "You're just an incredible snoop who can't help herself."

"You figured all this out?" I said.

"I was getting close to putting it all together," Rooster said. "I only had my suspicions about your mom's boyfriend, but I was sure something was up with the guy who had the hots for you."

"I wouldn't say he had the hots for me," I said, blushing.

"Okay, Suzy, whatever you say," he said. "So, how are things going on the dog front?"

"They're great. How's that gorgeous German Shepherd puppy doing?"

"Titan's amazing," Rooster said. "And he's keeping my other one young."

"It's amazing what happens when you put a puppy with an older dog," I said.

"Yeah, and now that I've got the other ones out of the house, I can really focus on my shepherds," Rooster said, letting his comment hang in the air.

I was about to respond, then I frowned and stared at him.

"You're the one who dropped off the Dandie with her pups, aren't you?" I said.

"Bingo," he said, smiling.

"I'm thoroughly confused, Rooster."

"Kind of a nice break in the day, isn't it?" he said, laughing.

I laughed and sat down next to him on the snowmobile.

"But, how?"

"How did I come into possession of the Dandie?" he said.

"Yes."

"That's a very good question, Suzy."

"Thanks. I have my moments."

"It started around the holidays when we were having all the trouble with the Baxter Brothers," he said. "And then I happened to notice that they had a house guest staying with him. And then I also happened to notice the pair of Dandie Dinmont when they went outside to do their business one night."

"There were two of them?" I said.

"Yeah. But after the Baxter Brothers disappeared, I noticed that the other guy was also gone. I figured he'd just packed up and left for who knows where, but I decided to check the house just in case."

"And you found the dogs inside?" I said.

"Just the female," he said. "Then I figured either the male had gotten lost, or the guy had taken him with him. So I took the female home with me. And that's where she's been until I dropped her off at the Inn. I didn't even realize she was pregnant until she got a bit sluggish toward the end."

"Why didn't you drop her off earlier?" I said.

"I was going to do that the day I picked up Titan. I actually had her in my truck. But when I saw the male in one of your condos, I knew you were already somehow involved with those people or soon would be, and I decided to keep the female a bit longer to see how things played out. I figured that having her would give me some leverage in case I needed it."

"So they were planning on having a litter of puppies all along," I said.

"Either that or the male caught her in a weak moment," Rooster said, laughing. "I tell you, that Comann bunch is a weird collection of folks."

"How do you know about Comann?" I said, continuing to be baffled by my strange friend.

"Didn't I tell you the first time we talked about *those people*, that I'd come in contact with them once in the past and didn't ever want to do it again?"

"Yes, you did," I said. "Bill was somehow involved with the guy under the ice."

"He must have been," Rooster said. "The guy who had the two Dandies in the first place was long gone, and I can't think of anybody else it could have been."

"So Bill made the arrangements with your brother and cousin to steal the male from us?"

"That's what they told me," Rooster said. "But they never met face to face. It was all done over the phone and with wire transfers of the money."

"How much did they get for stealing the dog?" I said.

"A thousand bucks," Rooster said, shaking his head. "I would have given them two grand just to stay away from it."

"But they never called you," I said.

"No. My brother tends to live in my shadow. At least that's what he thinks. And he's bound and determined to do things on his own. But you probably noticed that he and my cousin are a couple inches short of a full meter."

I let the mixed metaphor pass without comment.

"Rooster, I need to ask you something."

"Sure."

"How did you help them escape from your camp?"

"Who says I helped them?" he said, giving me a coy smile.

"However you managed it, it was very clever. There weren't any tracks or a footprint in sight."

"Yeah, I have to admit I really enjoyed the conversation I had with Jackson and that detective. They were doing so much head scratching, they each needed two."

"Josie is convinced you used a helicopter," I said.

"I guess that makes some sense," he said. "What about you?"

"I don't think you needed a helicopter," I said.

"Oh, you don't, huh?" he said, staring at me.

"No. I did at first, but then I remembered you have *two* hunting camps near the quarry."

"Yeah, what about it?"

"Well, Rooster, we go way back, right?"

"Absolutely."

"And we have an agreement that while we look out for each other, we don't ask each other a lot of questions about certain things," I said.

226

"That's one of the things I like most about our friendship, Suzy."

"Me too," I said. "So what I will *say*, not ask, is that I wouldn't be surprised if you have some sort of tunnel that connects your two hunting camps. And I know why you would go to all that trouble."

"Because you never know when it might come in handy, right?" he said, grinning.

"Exactly. Do you remember telling me that a long time ago?"

"I certainly do," he said.

"Where are your brother and cousin?" I said.

"They're long gone," he said.

I blanched and stared at him.

"No, not long gone like the Baxter Brothers," he said, waving the idea away. "I gave them enough money to take an extended vacation with instructions to stay away for at least a year."

"That was nice of you," I said.

"Well, what can you do, right?"

"Sure, sure. Family."

"Yeah."

"Are you sure you don't want to stay for lunch? Chef Claire has worked her magic again."

"No, thanks. I need to get going," he said. "Nice shanty."

"All the comforts of home," I said.

"Say, I noticed you have a couple more flags up out there," he said.

I saw the binoculars on the seat of the snowmobile for the first time and peered through them. Four flags were flapping in the breeze.

"Chef Claire must be busy eating," I said, laughing.

"If you don't mind, I thought I'd head out there and see if I can catch a fish. I know you guys just throw them all back, and I'm in the mood for chowder."

"Knock yourself out, Rooster."

"What are you doing to do with the Dandie puppies?" he said.

"Probably watch two breeders fight for custody," I said, laughing. "Why, would you like one of them?"

"No, I'm fine with my two shepherds," he said, firing up his snowmobile. "Besides," he said, raising his voice to be heard over the roar of the engine, "I think they're really great dogs, but they come with a ton of baggage."

"Baggage?" I yelled.

"Yeah," he said. "Way too many historical underpinnings."

He roared off in search of hidden fish secured to flags flapping in the breeze and left me with an open-mouthed stare that soon became a grin.

Epilogue

Slowly, like a butterfly emerging from its cocoon, spring sprung. Then sprung a leak. The weather had turned warm, and the snow and ice began to melt. Then another storm arrived and dumped a final ten inches of snow. Josie and I cursed Mother Nature from the comfort of the living room, while Chef Claire took the opportunity to get in one final day of cross-country skiing. She hadn't even bothered to ask us to join her.

"Let's see," Josie said, scrolling through the menu on the TV. "We've got a romantic comedy starting in a couple of minutes that looks watchable."

"That'll do," I said taking a sip of coffee as I watched Chloe and Captain roll around in front of the fireplace. "I can't believe how big he's getting."

"Yeah, he's a bruiser," Josie said, smiling at her Newfie.

My phone rang, and I recognized Jackson's number. I set the phone down on the coffee table and put it on speaker.

"Good morning, Jackson," I said.

"Hi, guys," Jackson said, then paused.

"Chef Claire isn't here," I said.

"Oh, I thought she might be home given the storm," he said.

"She went cross-country," Josie said.

"With Freddie?" he said.

"Your powers of deduction continue to fire on all cylinders," Josie said. "Who was it that said they were worried they might be fading?"

"That would be you, Josie," he said. "Are you done?"

"I'm done," she said, glancing at me. "He's just not as much fun these days."

"I know," I said, laughing. "You need to lighten up, Jackson."

"Yeah, either that or I need new friends."

"There you go," Josie said. "That's our guy."

"What's up?" I said.

"You won't believe what we just found along the shore," Jackson said.

"Jackson, I'm pretty burned out on solving mysteries at the moment so why don't you just tell me?"

"One of the Baxter Brothers," he said.

Josie turned the TV off, and we both focused on the phone.

"A floater?" I said.

"Well, he wasn't really floating per se," he said. "He was kinda bouncing off the rocks if you get my drift."

"Yuk," Josie said.

"Which one was it?" I said.

"I think it's Bobby, but it's a bit hard to tell at the moment."

"So he was under the ice all winter?" I said.

"That's my guess," he said. "But we'll have to wait until Freddie gets a look at him. Hey, that reminds me. I need to call Freddie. Now that is a phone call I'm going to enjoy."

Jackson cackled on the other end of the line.

"Just try not to enjoy ruining his day skiing too much. It might rub Chef Claire the wrong way," Josie said.

"Good point," Jackson said. "You'll never guess what we found on the body in a million years."

I thought about it for a minute, then smiled.

"It wasn't a big stack of hundreds by any chance was it?" I said, remembering Millie telling us about the thick wad of cash the guy under the ice had been carrying when he'd been in the bar with the Baxter Brothers.

"How on earth did you know that?" Jackson said, stunned.

"Lucky guess," I deadpanned.

"Okay, smarty pants," he said. "Guess what else we found?"

"I'm sorry, Jackson," I said. "I think I'm going to quit while I'm ahead."

"The wallet of the guy we found under the ice," Jackson said.

"Interesting. Was there any ID?" I said, glancing at Josie.

"Tons. And not just IDs. I've got photos."

"What was his name?" I said.

"Are you ready for this? Wilbur Wild."

I was stunned by the news.

"Wild. As in like William Wild?"

"That's where the photos come in," Jackson said. "They were brothers. I have one photo of them taken when they were young. And another one that looks fairly recent."

"Are there any photos of the parents?" Josie said.

"I have an old photo of a young couple that I guess could be the parents. But there aren't any with the kids and the adults together," Jackson said.

"Brothers?" Josie said, frowning.

"Not just brothers," I said. "Orphans. Sent to different orphanages when they were young."

"And then they were reunited through Comann?" Josie said. "That's too weird."

"It certainly is," I said. "Do you remember when Wentworth said there was no way that Bill could have killed the guy under the ice?"

"Yeah," Josie said. "I just thought he was referring to Bill not being in the area when it happened."

"I thought the same thing," I said. "But he couldn't do it because of the family connection."

"Hey, guys," Jackson said. "I need to run."

"Thanks for calling, Jackson," I said.

"Invite me to dinner, and I promise to tell you all about it," he said.

"You got it," I said. "Cocktail hour starts at six."

"See you then," he said, ending the call.

"Are you okay?" Josie said, sitting back in her chair.

"Yeah, I think so," I said. "But I think I might take a walk."

"Sure. We'll catch another movie later on."

"No, you go ahead," I said. "I shouldn't be long. What do you say, Chloe? Feel like going for a walk?"

Chloe hopped up and headed for the door. Captain followed her into the kitchen.

"I'll just take Captain along if he wants to go," I said.

"Sure."

I grabbed my coat and opened the kitchen door. A small windblown pile of snow filled the doorway. I shook my head at winter for the fifth time since I'd gotten up and swept the snow back out onto the porch, then mopped the floor dry. I started out the door, but Chloe and Captain remained sitting on the doorstep.

"You don't want to go for a walk?" I said.

Chloe barked once, then wagged her tail and headed back into the living room with Captain trailing close behind.

"You're both cowards," I said, laughing as I walked outside.

The wind had picked up and was blowing the snow in a swirling pattern that once again reminded me of a childhood memory about cotton candy. I trudged down the shoveled path until I reached the back edge of our property that extended off the far end of the dog's play area. I headed for the small stand of pine trees hoping to discover a semblance of the winter wonderland we'd seen the morning after our adventure at Rooster's hunting camp.

But I was done with winter and any solace I found came solely from the fact that I was alone and had some time to think. I leaned against one of the pines and studied the snow-covered branches and boughs and the pattern of the wind as it wound its way through the trees. I brushed snow off my shoulders and arms and focused on the silence that surrounded me.

My phone rang, and I thought about letting it go to voice mail. But I checked the number, one I didn't recognize and answered on the third ring.

"This is Suzy."

"Hi. It's me."

"William?"

"Just call me Bill," he said, chuckling. "How are you?"

"Actually, I'm feeling a little disoriented at the moment," I said. "I just heard fifteen minutes ago that it looks like we found out who killed... your brother."

I waited out a long silence, then he finally responded.

"How did you know Wilbur was my brother?" he said.

"The floater they found this morning had your brother's ID and family photos on him. Along with a big stack of cash."

"I always tried to warn him about flashing a lot of money around. But he never listened. Who killed him?"

"A couple of local reprobates that aren't worth discussing," I said. "You knew it was your brother all along, didn't you?"

"Yeah, I figured it out," he said.

"And you decided to stick around until you did, right?" I said, holding the phone tight.

"At first, yeah," he said. "And then I met you."

I fought back the tears and blamed the wind.

"Another lie?" I said.

"No, I think you're amazing," he said. "And we could have been great."

"Maybe," I said, composing myself. "You were orphaned and sent to separate orphanages. Then you somehow got reunited through Comann, right?"

"Yeah, those orphanages exist to identify potential recruits. I guess, as brothers, we both fit the job description of what the society looks for."

"And then your brother brought you into Wentworth's company," I said.

"Yes," he said. "Wentworth's already out on bail."

"I heard. Apart from pulling a gun on us, I'm not exactly sure if he did anything illegal while he was here," I said, finally verbalizing something that had been rolling around in my head since the ice fishing incident.

"He didn't have anything to do with Wilbur's death or the theft of your dog if that's what you're getting at. And he's probably going to skate," he said.

"Even though he infiltrated the FBI?" I said.

"I doubt if many people are going to be talking about that, especially the FBI. I'm sure they're very embarrassed about it, and Wentworth knows where all the skeletons are buried. Funny how all that works, huh?"

"Funny isn't the word I'd use," I said.

"Yeah, well. It's a different world from the one you live in, Suzy. Wentworth is really an amazing guy. My brother worshiped him."

"And I'm willing to bet that your brother was the one who lobbied for your recent promotion."

"You know a lot," he said.

"Is that going to be a problem for me?" I whispered.

"No. You don't have to worry about that," he said. "And that is definitely not a lie."

"Okay, thanks. I appreciate that."

"This is harder than I thought it would be," he said.

"You'll get over it," I said. "Whose idea was it to steal the two Dandies and produce a litter?"

"Wilbur came up with that one after he got thrown out," he said.

"Thrown out of Comann?"

"Yeah. Wilbur was adamant about how it was time for him to move into the elite ranks. And then he talked me into getting that stupid tattoo. All it did was put more heat on both of us."

"It sounds like a pretty stupid thing to do," I said.

"Well, it sounded good at the time," he said.

"Let me guess," I said. "Alcohol may have been involved."

He laughed, and it sounded great. And it broke my heart.

"After he got thrown out, Wilbur met a couple of guys who said they had some dog smuggling ring operating up the Islands and that they'd be able to provide cover for him until the litter was ready. So after he stole both dogs, that's what he did."

"He stole the one in Scotland as what, some form of weird payback to the orphanage over there?"

"It was something like that. When Wilbur did his research on the top Dandie breeders, he learned that one of them was located a couple of miles from where he'd grown up. He couldn't resist the irony."

"And your parents?"

"A classic tale of family destruction," he said, trying to sound casual, but coming across as still haunted by the memory. "Father loves to drink. Father loves to smack mother around when he's hammered. Mother decides she's finally had enough and tries to fight back. Father beats mother to death."

"You weren't there to see it were you?" I stammered.

"Oh, yeah," he whispered. "I was eight. Wilbur was seven."

A stream of tears ran down my cheeks.

"What happened to your father?"

"He took off and somehow managed to disappear. That is until I tracked him down a couple of years ago," he said. "Let's just say it wasn't the happiest of reunions for him and leave it at that."

"I'm so sorry," I finally managed.

"Hey, one door closes, another one opens, right?" he said, exhaling loudly into the phone.

"So where are you?" I said.

"I can't tell you that, Suzy."

"Okay. Then what are you going to do?"

"I'm going to follow in my father's illustrious footsteps and go into hiding for a very long time," he said.

"Do you think they will come looking for you?"

"I'm sure they already are," he said. "But they won't find me. I've been trained to deal with situations like this. And they know it. They'll go through the motions for a while, then they'll quit."

"Unless you resurface," I said.

"Which I won't."

I gulped and coughed.

"But I sure wish I could," he said. "You're an amazing woman, Suzy."

"I'm not so sure about amazing," I said. "But I'm definitely snoggable."

"Absolutely," he said, laughing. "You're off the charts snoggable."

"At least I've got that going for me," I said, finally finding my laugh.

"Good luck on that search for total consciousness," he said.

Score a point for Just Call Me Bill. Not everybody got that movie reference.

"Look, I need to go," he said. "If I get a chance at some point in the future, would it be okay if Wild Bill gave you a call?"

"No," I whispered as a fresh round of tears filled my eyes.

"Yeah, I get it," he said, eventually. "Okay, you take good care of yourself, Suzy."

"You, too. Try to have a good life… William."

I slid the phone back in my pocket, opened my wet, misty eyes as far as I could, then turned around and let the wind have its way with me.

Made in the USA
Lexington, KY
25 January 2017